Two Once Removed

by
Milo Hays

www.milohays.com

ISBN-13: 978-1-7353404-0-1

Cover design by: Milo Hays
Printed in the United States of America

## 1

It was an unexpected fun Saturday night on what should have been an otherwise boring fall Outer Banks beach weekend. The warm glow of the setting North Carolina sun enhanced the richness of their rejuvenated tans as the sounds of Bob Marley and the Wailers circulated with the onshore breeze. The pounding surf supported the forecast that their perfect October summer-like weather was about to change.

The families gathered on the sand for cocktail hour proudly called themselves the *Abbies*. Short for Aborigines, no one knew exactly when or who started the happy-hour revelry that often lasted well into the evenings. It was established generations ago by some of the original families who built and owned oceanfront cottages that were later handed down through the generations that followed.

The friendships forged in this group strengthened over decades as children grew up to become parents, then grandparents. Their allegiances were strong. Their suspicion of new owners looking to change their piece of heaven was always immediate.

Jason Cartwright was the newest owner to join the usually closed festivities that ran almost nightly through the summer, less frequently in September, and only occasionally as weather and participation would permit in October. He was also a very rare new owner *welcome* to the group, having bought one of the remaining, never-available cottages out of an estate earlier in the year.

The price Jason paid for his new home set a record as he had to outbid a number of highly motivated buyers thought of as 'unfriendlies' by the Abbies. 'Unfriendlies' were new owners that tore down old cottages to build monstrosities limited only by the community's property-line setbacks. Jason was the only unknown bidder in the group. Their hope fell to him to save one of the few remaining gems on the strand.

At first, both sides were standoffish as the Abbies waited to see what Jason was planning to do. His surprising plan to rehabilitate the old, dilapidated wood cottage back to its old glory opened conversations that created new friendships and welcomed him into the group.

Jason's rare acceptance by the old guard also turned out to be a godsend. It offered immediate friendships that created a desperately needed sense of family for the recently divorced and relocated fifty-five-year-old father of two college and two adult daughters. His move to the shore was to find relief away from the company he just sold and his hometown of Cleveland. Both offered many great opportunities to him through his life and for his family. But it was time for something new. His divorce was his release from his obligation to stay. He knew the beach was a place where his kids would make an effort to visit.

As the sun drifted slowly behind the row of homes that lined the horizon, Jason worked his way through the crowd to say goodnight to his friends. His experience over the summer told him they would still be there partying long after darkness surrounded them. That was their tradition; the nearing end of their extended season was their added motivation to enjoy every single minute.

So, on the unusually warm night that was blessed by an onshore breeze that kept the bugs away, the setting was nirvana; and this party was long from over. But, as much as he wanted to stay, Jason had a pressing matter that was long overdue and growing extremely time sensitive.

"Where are you heading? The party's just getting started," Celeste Regus asked in her low, raspy Southern accent while taking a firm hold of his arm.

Celeste was a direct descendent of one of the original families whose presence dated back to the 1800s. Divorced for over ten years, she worked hard to keep her forty-five-year-old figure fit and taut while always surveying the horizon for male companionship.

Celeste knew Jason's history, having immediately dug into his public social media accounts and exhausting Google when she heard his bid for the cottage was accepted. What she uncovered was perfect reconnaissance for her summer approach. She made a special effort to be on the island and to be one of the first to meet him when he arrived in late spring. But her enthusiasm receded when she met the then-tired and heavier version of the current person. His final, long, cold Ohio winter, that included finalizing his divorce and the sale of his company, nearly finished him. Her disinterest, however, did not last long.

Celeste's impression of him changed when Jason's immediate efforts to trim down started to produce the results that created the desired physical package she wanted. As that happened, she went back on the hunt to position herself near him during regular cocktail hours as well as to look for him on the beach for the 'coincidental' stroll-by conversation.

"Celeste. Heyyy," Jason replied, stumbling through his words while trying to gently work his arm free.

The verbal fumble was half caused by his slight inebriation and half by surprise from the last-second grab of his arm.

"I'm just on my way back to the cottage to do some work."

"Work can wait," Celeste declared, moving close to him. "It's party time."

Jason smiled at the invitation. Celeste's clock was always 'party time.' He was forewarned about her by some of the others in the group who knew her life history. Until this moment, he had successfully steered clear of her approaches.

"I'm sorry," he replied as he freed himself of her grip. "This is very important to me and very time sensitive. I've also been procrastinating on it for a couple months now."

Celeste was not taking the hint and started to walk with him as he tried to continue his escape.

"I'm very time sensitive too, Jason," she replied while trying to maintain soft eye contact. "I may be gone for the season after tonight."

Her comment caused Jason to stop and to think.

"I hope not," he responded with a sad smile and in his most pleasing voice. "I'll miss seeing you. But, have a great winter and new year if this is goodbye."

Celeste deflated to his dismissal of her proposition. Her shoulders dropped as her happy anticipation left her face. Feeling responsible, Jason placed his cooler in the sand and his drink on top of it. He gave her a brief embrace before releasing to recollect his things. As he let go, Celeste tried to pull him closer with the most inviting eyes she could manage. Jason smiled warmly at her continued effort, then gently eased out of her particularly tight hold to make his way off into the darkening twilight.

# # #

The revelry from the party continued as the moon hovered above the water. Its light reflected off the rolling surf and shoreline to create the perfect romantic ambiance. Jason, however, was not listening. He was lost in thought staring at his laptop, now finally satisfied with his effort.

Jason's favorite place to be and to work was on the bench alcove built into the elevated walkway that connected his cottage to the barrier dune that protected all the homes from the ocean. Stairs that dropped directly down to the beach completed the walkway. The view from the bench captured the ocean north and south as far as the eye could see. It also was far enough forward to give sightlines on neighboring homes up and down the shoreline.

Jason could feel the breeze off the water getting cooler. It felt good and kept the bugs from buzzing around his screen. He took a sip of Bulleit bourbon from the tumbler he had next to him as he considered what he was about to do. He knew he had to finish his effort tonight. The season was almost over.

As he took a second, bigger sip of bourbon, he grew more confident in the pictures he had chosen. His phone held hundreds of photos dating from the time of the cottage's purchase, through its renovations, and up to its near completion now. He also had other shots from the summer that he had either taken himself or received from others. A few, however, were immediately discarded as not suited for public display, as they were taken toward the tail end of some of the Abbies' happier happy hours that got a little out of hand.

For his final upload, Jason chose four photos. The first was of the dilapidated cottage he purchased as it stood on the day he bought it. The second was from the same angle taken a day ago to show the transformation of the property through the summer. The third picture was a beautiful panoramic photo taken by his daughter Maya from the deck bench that showed the ocean at sunrise. The fourth and final picture was of him, tan and skinny, standing at the handrail by the bench at sunset, keeping a watchful look out over the water. Jason was hesitant to include a picture of him, tending to not like any photo of him ever taken. This one, however, worked.

The caption for his Facebook post read

Ready for Visitors. Anytime.

As a regular viewer of Facebook, a sometimes commenter, and a rare poster, Jason's view of social media was that it enabled old friends to connect without having to get together. The advertisements and other clutter were just gloss-over. Facebook was his tool to find and reconnect with those from his past who wanted to connect again with him.

"It's now or never, Brownie," he proclaimed ceremoniously to his three-year-old Chesapeake Bay retriever, Zoe, who was curled up at his feet.

He placed the cursor arrow over the *post* button. The click seemed amplified as his invitation disappeared from his screen, giving him an exhilarating conflict between anxiousness and relief wondering if anyone would come. His divorce took a toll on many of his 'friendships' from home. His daughters were all busy in their collegiate and post-collegiate lives. He had many friends from long ago up and down the coast that he wanted to see again. But everyone was busy, and calendars were tight. Except his. Having sold his company a year ago, Jason was free to enjoy life for its offerings.

As he closed his laptop, he left just the moon to illuminate the setting around him. It was a peace he loved and knew he wanted to share.

## 2

Friday's weather forecast for the Washington, DC suburb of Great Falls, Virginia was encouraging. Despite rain having saturated the East Coast for the past few days, the latest forecast had the sun returning Saturday morning to be followed by three beautiful days of sunny fall weather. Columbus Day weekend was not going to be a washout.

The dramatic shift in weather was welcome news to Chase Larson, who had been watching the forecasts closely as he politicked from parish to parish through Louisiana for the past two weeks. At fifty-three, he was one of the Republican Party's most sought-after campaign advisors. But these engagements required tours that were exhausting and constantly kept him away from home for weeks on end. This senatorial tour was particularly tiring. He was ready for the fun and relaxation that was waiting for him this weekend.

Chase arrived home to Virginia early Friday afternoon after taking an early morning flight that connected through and lost valuable time in Atlanta. He had just enough time to pack and to get on the road for his three-day golf weekend with his college buddies.

The weekend that was planned was special. It was their thirtieth college anniversary that had to be commemorated with an overload of alcohol and golf, just like their twenty-ninth and the other twenty-eight that preceded them. This trip was their boy's weekend tradition that usually did not fall on Columbus Day weekend and never once included the wives.

As Chase gathered food and drink from the chef's kitchen of his Northern Virginia McMansion, Callie, his wife of twenty-five years, was dealing with an unexpected call from their daughter, Lizzie, who continued to struggle as a new college freshman.

"Lizzie, I know you're not having any fun yet," she said sympathetically into her cell. "But you have to stay on campus to meet people. Your brothers went through the same thing."

Although she was doing her best to stay understanding to the situation, Callie was losing her patience. Not with Lizzie, who was having very real problems adjusting to college. But with Chase, who had prioritized getting on the road to his golf weekend over helping either his daughter cope with college or his wife try to calm the situation.

Chase's drive to his weekend at the Battlefields Resort near Richmond was going to be just over two hours in good traffic. It included a long stretch on I-95 south with all the other DC commuters who would likely be heading out early for their holiday weekends with their families. Chase knew the later he started, the worse the bumper-to-bumper interstate traffic would be, and the later he would arrive. Callie knew this too. But, to her, there was no rush for him to get going when more pressing matters involving their child were front and center.

"Lizzie? Your dad is packing up and about to leave."

Callie paused to decipher Lizzie's crying response. She was near hysteria and not listening.

"No, you can't come home this weekend," she quickly interjected into an unexpected pause. "Fall break is next weekend. We'll see you then."

Callie pulled the phone away from her ear and put it on speaker. After turning up the volume, she extended it towards Chase for him to hear his daughter's anguish. Lizzie's ongoing emotional appeal echoed through the room. Callie's deal-with-it face to her husband expressed more clearly the need for him to step up than any words she could say.

Chase listened for a moment, then surveyed Callie to take a temperature on her disposition. Using her eyes, she directed him to take the phone to console their daughter. But he waved her off, leaving her to manage the crisis. Callie was the family's soother. After waiting a brief moment to get nothing, Callie angrily pulled the phone back and Chase resumed packing his cooler.

"Lizzie? Sweetie? Find something fun to do tonight with your suite mates. You have the football game tomorrow. It'll be a good weekend."

Callie made the suggestion, not knowing what Lizzie had said moments before. She then began to show relief when her daughter finally agreed to stay at school for the weekend. She also felt a growing comfort that Lizzie's emotional tirade was over for now.

"I'll call you tomorrow after the game," Callie added to fill the silence.

"Bye, Lizzie!" Chase shouted from across the room.

As Callie placed her phone on the counter, she sat silently glaring at Chase. Although sad and concerned for Lizzie, she was furious with her husband. Their last child, and only daughter, was having difficulty adapting to college. Yet, all he was concerned about was what drinks and snacks to pack for his road trip.

"I should've let her come home," she finally remarked after Chase stayed silent.

"Absolutely not," he responded. "She's eighteen years old and needs to separate from home. That's the way my family did it."

"She's our baby," Callie responded, hoping that one point of reference would get him to see the coldness of his statement. "And your parents sent you off to boarding school in the ninth grade."

"Proves my point even more. I turned out just fine."

Chase snapped the finish of the zipper on his cooler with a wash of his hand to emphasize that as his closing point on the matter.

"Yeah, well that's debatable," Callie quipped back. "You can be so fucking cold."

Chase absorbed the hit undaunted. Callie was mad about the golf weekend long before Lizzie called and amplified things further. It was a no-win situation. He set his bags and cooler next to the door to the garage and took one last look around the kitchen. Noting nothing of consequence, he bent down to make his escape.

"So. You're just going to go?" she asked just as his grip tightened on the bag handles.

Callie intentionally waited and timed the question to that moment. She knew it would piss him off. Twenty-five years of marriage had uncovered all the buttons to push. His chubby physique from endless business travel and bad food was always a sore spot too, when she needed it. But for now, her goal was to delay him in order to put him deeper and deeper into the rush-hour traffic that was building on I-95. She knew it. And he knew exactly what she was doing.

As Chase straightened to respond, Callie moved from the island bar stool to the comfort of the breakfast-area bay window. Chase watched her change locations as he configured his response. His job as a political campaign consultant gave him expertise with in-the-moment responses. As she rested her fit, five-foot-four, fifty-year-old physique on the cushions in front of the window, she looked over their manicured front yard and driveway. It was her favorite perch to relax when able. Her kids and the dog loved it too when either waiting for meals or a ride somewhere.

"It's just a weekend," he answered with a dismissive tone.

He knew he was not going to win this argument. He just wanted to get going. He even considered conceding everything if he knew she would let him go. Callie let his comment stand for a moment, waiting for more. Nothing came.

"Seriously?!" she said with a glare that meant business. "You've just been away for two weeks... and... you're traveling a ton through Thanksgiving. I think I'll see you maybe ten days... rather likely only nights... during that time."

"I do have to work," he answered coldly.

Chase was irritated by the insinuation that his travels were his choice and was losing sympathy for his wife's needs. His entire career involved travel, which she knew going in. And it was never a problem, until now.

"That's not my point and you know it," she responded. "I don't even know where you are or who you are with most of the time that I'm just stuck here."

Callie knew the insinuation that he could be cheating would sting. Despite his job taking him out of the area on a regular basis for long periods of time, Callie had never hinted, let alone stated, she ever thought he was unfaithful. Chase absorbed the hit again without flinching, as his years of campaigning had weathered him to do. As he walked toward her, Callie neither looked away nor blinked.

"I keep in touch with you when I'm away," he argued. "You know who I'm with. This weekend was planned last winter. I'm also entitled to one fucking weekend with my friends as a reward for everything I do to bring in money to support this house, you, and the kids."

"It's not about the money," Callie shot back. "It's about us. We do not spend any time together anymore. The kids are GONE. I gave up my career to raise them. My life is empty... and you'd rather golf than be with me."

Chase paused to think. He knew she was right. But he needed to find an 'out' to the situation that did not sacrifice his weekend. He also knew she would make it through the weekend for time together on a later date. He could have both.

"Why don't you call your friends for a girls' night out?" he blurted without much thought.

Chase's mood lightened with the thought he had just made a great suggestion. She could duplicate his selfish weekend with her friends. Even if for just one night, it would be enough for everything to be good again. She could not be upset with his weekend of fun if she had one of her own. But to his surprise, Callie did not either move or respond. She just sat still while shaking her head in disbelief.

"Because...." she replied in a slow, dead-pan tone to convey the stupidity of his suggestion, "they're all busy with their spouses and families over the holiday weekend. Like NORMAL COUPLES and families who LOVE EACH OTHER!"

Callie's slow emphasis of her point showed signs of working. Chase now understood what she had been saying about being left home alone again. But his sympathy for his wife's predicament was not going to override and ruin his free and fun weekend with his friends. He knew he could fix whatever damage leaving now would cause. He had done it before. He was certain this issue was just like the others that could be fixed the next time he was home and over the holidays when all the kids were around.

"I'll make it up to you," he replied.

His tone was half genuine and half desperate to get some blend of permission to leave and forgiveness for putting his friends over his wife.

Callie finally broke eye contact with him. Looking at the floor, she responded quietly as their five-year-old Cocker Spaniel, Molly, jumped to join her. She cuddled next to Callie, who started to stroke her to feel some affection from somewhere.

"No, Chase. No, you won't. You know what? Just fucking go. Molly and I will find something fun to do this weekend. We always do. Maybe this time, we'll go looking for a man who wants to be with me instead of just married to me."

Callie's tone was raw and full of defeat. It also was loaded with truth. Chase did not like the threat. She had never said anything close to that, even in more heated moments. His thirty years in political campaign management made him exceptionally good at telling a bluff from a threat. Callie's words were not a bluff. And that concerned him. But, more so, he was angry with her for even suggesting she would be unfaithful to him.

"What the hell do you mean by that!?"

"Just go," she answered. "If you can't figure it out, then just go."

Callie was not backing down; and she was done explaining. Her voice was defiant. She did not lift her eyes to look at him. Callie knew there was no convincing him not to go and that it was time to give up. Her plan now was to sting him as hard as possible before he left so that his two-hour drive, that hopefully had become four, would be enough windshield time for her words to sink in to convince him to turn around.

Chase stayed silent as he turned and walked toward the garage. He stopped for a moment to look at his bags. He was hoping for Callie's reassurance that it was OK for him to go. He did not get it. She was not even looking at him. He walked back past her to grab napkins he did not need to get her attention. She continued to look away. He then kissed her lightly on the top of her head to get no reaction. After waiting a moment longer, Chase left her side and walked straight to the garage. He grabbed his bags and the cooler, waiting for another, well-timed comment that did not come. As he stepped through the doorway in total silence, he stopped.

"I'll let you know when I get there," he said, hoping for something.

Callie did not respond as she continued to stroke the dog. He waited a moment longer as she continued to ignore him. He then disappeared into the garage. The sound of the garage door opening told Callie that his decision to go was final until he reappeared in the doorway.

"Why don't you visit your mother in Williamsburg?" he suggested. "Maybe have dinner with Will while you're there?"

Punched again, Callie shook her head while calmly reminding him that it was William and Mary's homecoming weekend. Will, their second child, a junior, would be busy. Chase showed indifference to the fact he did not remember as he just turned and left.

As the kitchen door to the garage clicked shut, Callie looked up to find the room empty. The distinct high-revving sound of Chase's Maserati starting filled the air around her. It was a sound she used to find amusing and exhilarating. The distinct engine noise grew louder as he backed out of the garage and became even louder as he accelerated out the driveway through the rain.

Callie intentionally looked away as the blue blur of his car appeared in the window through her peripheral vision. Chase double-tooted the horn as he swept by. It was a habit from when they were not fighting. Likewise, Callie responded with a wave. But this time with her middle finger erect and directed towards the car. When she could no longer hear his engine, she hugged Molly for comfort.

Having no prospects for the weekend, Callie looked around at her large, empty kitchen that was the centerpiece of the McMansion she used to love. What used to be filled with the chaos of three kids, their friends, and endless activities was now dead silent. The only noise of note was the refrigerator's hum, which she never noticed before but bothered her now for the first time.

Sadness further encased Callie as she realized that this emptiness was now her new normal. Chase's extended business travel that had gone unnoticed in the past when Callie was managing kid craziness was not going to stop. The absence of her children, now in college, had created a vacuum in her life that was now very real and could not be easily filled. The dreary day and rain outside darkened her mood further as she stared out the window into the distant neighborhood. Molly was content to be the center of her attention as time just drifted. Callie had just reached complete numbness when her phone started singing and vibrating.

The dedicated ringtone immediately identified the caller as her childhood friend Sandy Worth. A friend from their shared hometown of Cleveland, Sandy, like so many others, also moved to DC after college and never left.

"What?" Callie answered, with an unusually direct and unfriendly tone that was half sarcastic and half not.

"Geez, don't be crabby. It's Columbus Day weekend!" Sandy opened with a nauseating happiness in her voice. "Do you have your cell handy?"

Callie pulled her phone from her ear and looked at it in disbelief.

"I'm talking to you on it," she replied.

"Oh, right. Put me on speaker and go to my Facebook."

Callie pulled the phone down and pressed the glass face to switch to speaker. She then found and pushed the Facebook icon to load Sandy's page onto her screen. Her face went blank.

"First mate's single again. And he's alone at the beach," Sandy declared in a gleeful tone.

Callie scrolled through the week-old post by Jason Cartwright. Jason and Callie were engaged to be married twenty-seven years ago. It was a wedding that did not happen that was the talk of their community in Cleveland as their engagement ended abruptly six weeks before the ceremony. Although they dated briefly afterward to figure things out, Callie ended the relationship for good seeing no hope and, more so, for not getting any answers. Jason soon after moved away without warning. Callie followed with her own move back to DC almost a year later.

There was no parting discussion to resolve anything between the two before they both headed in different directions. They only spoke once, which was soon after Jason had moved. Their discussion showed promise, then quickly died off again.

Jason drove Callie back to her apartment after they accidentally crossed paths at their club swimming pool in Cleveland. He was home for the weekend and was heading out that evening. The short ride turned into a lengthy conversation that ended in the early evening with an emotional hug Jason could still feel today.

Jason heard about Callie's wedding through friends who provided details well beyond what he either needed or wanted to know. It was painful to hear. But he never stopped them from talking.

The only break of the absolute silence that followed was ten years ago when Jason wrote Callie a condolence letter months after hearing her father had died. The letter focused on her dad with no mention of them except for the honor he felt when her dad gave his permission to Jason to ask Callie to marry him.

Beyond that one unanswered contact, the two lived separate lives with spouses and children that each would see only when secretly snooping on the other's Facebook pages and posts. Neither ever attempted to post toward the other when on a common friend's page. Mutual respect had created a wall between them without either conferring with the other to build it.

"So, what!" Callie blurted out, appearing upset with the poorly timed life interjection of a topic they usually joked about. "I also doubt he's alone. And I'm really not in the mood for this."

Callie's tone was raw and sharp, like her mood.

"Besides, I told you calling him 'first mate' wasn't funny anymore."

"Callie's first mate? That's hilarious!" Sandy replied, not realizing humoring herself was insensitive to her friend's feelings.

Callie ran her fingers through her hair in frustration. She was trying to tell her friend nicely not to be such an *unfeeling bitch*. From what Callie had said many times about her loneliness, Sandy should have known that she was hurting. Callie looked to end the conversation.

"It's just not a good time for this," she said. "I just had it out with Chase about his golf weekend. I'm just so fucking tired of being left here alone while he gets to gallivant off."

Sandy did not immediately respond, now realizing Callie was truly troubled.

"Are you OK?"

"Peachy," she answered sarcastically with her usual pissed-off reflex. "Besides, it's been over twenty-five years since he bailed on me. I really don't care what he's doing now or who he's 'doing' for that matter. In fact, I hope he fucking drowns in the rip currents."

"Don't be angry," Sandy answered. "I was just trying to lighten your holiday weekend Friday. I forgot about the golf trip."

Callie exhaled heavily to clear her head. It was all too much coming at her at the same time. She took another look at the picture of Jason.

"He's thin now," she said in a surprised tone. "He was such a porker for the longest time. Got the salt and pepper thing going too. He looks good."

Callie studied the photos more closely, then laughed.

"That place is a dump. Look at all that construction crap everywhere."

"That's my girl! She's back!" Sandy giggled. "You know what!? We should take a road trip to check him out from a distance. Just a drive-by. It's only five hours. We can do a beach nearby. You've got time now with Chase traveling and Lizzie at school."

Callie laughed to herself internally pondering the suggestion, then returned to her senses.

"I'll tell you what. Why don't you take the road trip? And if he sees you, which I'm sure he will, challenge him to swim with the sharks."

"You can't still hate him that much," Sandy replied, having realized the insensitivity of her suggestion.

Callie held her answer as she welled up with emotion. Her exhaustion from the day was reaching its limit. Most of it because of her frustration with Lizzie and her battle with Chase. But the final straw was Sandy's presentation that her first love was again single, available, and posting for people to visit him at the beach. He was looking for someone to be with.

"Look, I'm about to head out to my mom's," Callie stated strongly, as she continued to study the photos. "This has been lovely... really. But I have to get out of here before my head explodes."

"That's perfect!" Sandy exclaimed, excited to hear about her friend's imminent trip to Williamsburg. "You'll be just two hours from him. Hell, I'd do the drive for just a look. Aren't you curious? Just a bit?"

"Not happening," Callie replied quickly. "I can see him on Facebook if I want to snoop then swipe him away. That's enough."

Callie became more incensed as she thought through Sandy's suggestion.

"You can go," she finished. "But, if you do, I never want to hear about it.... ever!"

Sandy giggled at Callie's fired-up stance to what she felt was only a hypothetical opportunity to revisit the past.

"Ok. But... you will tell me if YOU go. Right?"

Sandy sensed a tinge of curiosity that just may be enough to entice Callie to go during her open weekend.

"Say hi to your mom for me... And also to Jayy-sonn... If you see him, of course. BYYYEEE."

Sandy hung up quickly before Callie could respond. After taking a deep breath, Callie did find some humor in the absurdity of Sandy's idea. That trip would truly make Chase think about leaving her again for a weekend. But Jason Cartwright was twenty-seven years ago. She was likely old news to him as a distant, young and naïve triumph.

As she packed for the long weekend in Williamsburg, she remained intrigued by the potential of secretly seeing Jason Cartwright and maybe even talking to him. The things she wanted to ask and to say to him were endless. She watched his four daughters grow up on Facebook over the past ten years. His girls were about the same ages as her kids. She also knew what his now-ex-wife looked like, which made her self-conscious. But more than anything, she wondered who he turned into through the experiences of life, marriage, work, and family. Callie knew she was much different from who she was when they loved each other. He certainly had to be too. She wondered if she would even like him today. And, on the flip side, if he wondered the same things about her.

Callie closed her roller suitcase to finish packing for her weekend visit with her mom. Visiting her mother unannounced could be either a fancy day of shopping and dining or just a relaxed day helping her in her garden. Callie had to have clothes for both. Williamsburg was around three hours in good traffic. Holiday traffic would make the drive longer. Molly was beginning to sense a road trip coming and did not leave Callie's side so she would not be left behind.

## 3

With the house alarm set, Callie pulled the door between the kitchen and garage shut. The garage door was already opened when she rolled her suitcase with Molly's family room dog bed on top of it to the car. All that was left was to load Molly into her usual spot on the front seat and to get on the road.

Callie climbed into her new Range Rover HSE. It was her fiftieth birthday present to replace a well-dressed five-year-old Chevy Suburban that she loved and really did not want to see go. Chase said the Range Rover celebrated her graduation from DC lacrosse-mom to full-time college-mom and empty-nester. That thought made her sad. But she went along with it because it made him happy and her kids envious. Callie also felt gratified that her having the Range Rover fulfilled his desire for her to have a car that made him seem less selfish, and to eliminate the torment she gave him about driving a Maserati.

Callie did one last look around to be sure she had everything she needed. Molly was settled in for the ride. The EZ-Pass was in place to ensure she could use the faster toll lanes on I-95 South instead of the congested free ones the common folks had to endure. Callie buckled her seat belt and started the car. As she backed out into the rain, the engine maintained its quiet hum as the wipers automatically turned on.

The drive to Williamsburg from Great Falls was going to be longer than usual. But the added time offered a lot of time to think, not to think, and hopefully not to overthink. She did not want to take her troubles with her. That would be a burden on her mother and ruin the weekend she needed to relax. Callie stopped in the driveway to find a good playlist on Spotify. She needed something light and fun to soothe her nerves in order to get through the heavy traffic and the rain.

# # #

As expected, the drive on I-95 south was congested and slow. The sun set just after 7:00 p.m. with less than an hour left in her trip. Her Spotify playlist was doing its job up until the music stopped abruptly to be replaced by a familiar ringtone that, up until now, made her happy. Without looking, Callie rejected Chase's call to let the music return. Surprisingly, nothing came after. Chase did not leave a voice message or send a text.

The rain eased to a misting drizzle as Callie exited the interstate near her mother's home. That was a good sign that maybe the wet lead-in to the weekend was finally giving way to the sunshine that had been promised. As she made her final turn, she saw her mother's familiar two-story house with its semicircle governor's driveway and impeccable landscaping. After parking in the driveway, Callie opened her door to feel a wash of wet, fresh October coolness that said fall was here.

Callie intentionally did not call in advance of her arrival. She was not sure if she would decide to turn around at any point in the trip, and calling ahead was never required. She wanted to have all the options on a guilt-free basis, even if Chase did not come to his senses and turn around. She was holding on to a small hope during her drive that he would call to say he was heading back home. By not answering his earlier call, she tested that hope. And when he did not leave either a message or send a text, she knew his call was just to say he had arrived safely.

Callie struggled with her bag, Molly, and the dog bed as she made her way up to the front door. The door was unlocked, giving them both immediate entry. As they walked into the quiet front hall, Callie placed her bag by the door and dropped the dog bed beside it. Molly scampered toward the kitchen as she normally did to look for food. Callie began to look for her mom.

"Mom?" she called out as she peeked into the adjacent living and dining rooms.

"Callie?" replied a voice from down below.

Callie could hear the sound of steps coming from the basement stairs that led to the kitchen. She moved to kitchen to greet her mom as she emerged from the top of the stairs.

Carolyn's house was modern contemporary construction, built in the late 1990s to impeccable standards. It had expansive casual space that Callie's dad wanted when he and Carolyn retired from Cleveland to Williamsburg twenty years ago. The bay windows that walled the back overlooked the James River from a high perch on the hill. It was a wonderful place for children to play, with lots of room inside to mellow their craziness. It also had more room outside to run them tired just before bedtime.

The evening hours were particularly peaceful with the water. The lights glowing off in the distance were hypnotic. There was rarely any noise beyond the sounds of nature when sitting on either the screened porch or in the sunroom overlooking the James.

Carolyn emerged from the basement carrying a small basket of freshly folded laundry. She was delighted and surprised to see Callie and Molly. Their phone call earlier in the week had Callie staying in DC for the weekend.

"Well, this is a pleasant surprise," Carolyn declared, while placing the basket on the kitchen's large island counter. She turned to hug Callie while looking down the hallway for her trailing husband. "Is Chase with you?"

Callie hesitated before shaking her head no. The mellow she achieved driving down and had walking into the comfort of her mother's home was all but erased by that single question. Carolyn had forgotten Callie's earlier complaints about Chase's annual boys-only weekend golf trip.

"No. He's golfing. Remember? I told you."

Carolyn's look of excitement immediately changed to sympathy. She knew the only reason Callie would make an unscheduled trip on a holiday weekend was that she was seeking some needed comfort for being left behind again.

"I've got just the thing," she said as her face lit.

Carolyn opened the door to her built-in Viking refrigerator to fetch a bottle of rosé.

"I just uncorked this an hour or so ago to have a glass. It was marvelous."

Callie found some humor in the comment and relief from her mother's attempt to divert her attention. It all seemed to be working. Not so much because they were having some wine together. But more because her mother was so enthusiastic about the wine-find she had just opened. 'Marvelous' was her dad's word when something was truly special. Callie retrieved some stemless glasses as Carolyn popped the cork, then intentionally filled each glass with a hearty pour.

"That certainly should do it," Callie smiled, acknowledging the generous first serving.

Carolyn answered by raising her glass for a silent toast. Each then took a healthy sip as they looked at each other. Carolyn was studying Callie's face and demeanor for signs of desperation. Callie was watching her mother's eyes scan over her while trying to maintain her composure through a look of happy contentment.

The two moved from the kitchen to settle into the sunroom that overlooked the river. The rain had restarted and was quietly streaking the floor-to-ceiling glass walls that showcased the view. Callie could feel her dad's presence. The room was his favorite place to rest and relax, particularly when the gardens were in bloom framing the river view. Over his final days, he would quietly admire his domain as he faded in and out of sleep up until the time came when he did not wake.

Carolyn knew the peace Callie felt in the room and intentionally kept their conversation to her three children while leaving out mention of her husband, who was selfishly off playing golf. Callie was aware and appreciative of her mom's effort. But she was also concerned about her problems entering Carolyn's sphere and their discussions. With Carolyn's age approaching eighty, Callie and her sisters agreed years ago to keep stress as far from her as possible. *Positive as Possible* was their *sister mantra* as it pertained to their mom.

"Your dad used to take boys' weekends too," Carolyn finally said to break an awkward silence. "Most of the time, I hated them. But, sometimes, they provided a nice break."

Callie was surprised by the comment. She listened respectfully as she looked out the window.

"Daddy didn't travel the way Chase does," she replied tactfully. "He's gone all the time and for long trips. I get my alone time during those times. Much more than I either want or need."

Carolyn smiled to offer a mother's understanding. Her comment did not soothe Callie as she had hoped. And Callie was right. Her father never traveled extensively for his job. His trips were occasional and only for a few days. It did not compare to the weeks of travel Chase took during campaign tours.

"You're absolutely right, sweetie," Carolyn said in a forgive-me tone. "Your dad's travel wasn't like Chase's."

Callie regretted making her mother feel bad and accepted her apology with a look of pained forgiveness.

"It was fine when the kids were growing up," she explained, knowing she was breaking the sisters' mantra. "There never was a moment to think. He was just either there or not there. I think it's probably bad to say I didn't even miss him when he wasn't there. I was exhausted at bedtime and back at it when the alarm rang to start the next day. Now there's nothing. And I want there to be SOMETHING. It's my time to be happy."

Callie's voice cracked as she finished. Her frustration and sadness had broken through her happy facade.

Carolyn knew there was nothing she could do to lift her daughter's spirits. That had to come from within and be supported by the like desires and actions of her husband. Through her own experience, Carolyn understood that men have to blow off steam every once in a while without their spouses. It rebuilds their testosterone and self-image. Perhaps even gives them an opportunity to bitch a little to someone who will listen. She saw Chase's weekend as potentially healthy for him and just poorly timed for Callie. Her concern, however, was for her daughter. A weekend in Williamsburg only offered a brief, and not terribly exciting, diversion rather than an end solution.

Callie remained to find peace in the dark sunroom long after Carolyn had gone to bed. The rain had slowed to a light drizzle as the lights started reappearing in the distance across the James. Callie's wine glass was empty before her mother said goodnight, and it remained empty as she did not have the desire to walk to the kitchen for a refill.

Williamsburg was always a comforting touchstone for Callie when life got stressful. Carolyn had a mother's touch to comfort and fix things that were wrong. But that touch started to fade as Callie got older and grandchildren appeared. Maybe that was because her problems weren't always in Carolyn's experience. Or maybe because the problems presented had solutions outside the realms of what Carolyn would ever think of or consider.

The peaceful cadence of the light rain on the window offered some relief as it helped pull Callie away from conscious thought. Her mind was adrift with an ease that was finally taking over her body when her phone lit and vibrated with a text tone. Callie looked to see an evaporating view of the message, then opened it.

I made it. Let me know what you do.

Callie stared at the words briefly wondering if and what she should respond. The text was his typical check-in. It was just a one-touch he did when traveling. It was also more than four hours after he likely arrived at his party. Callie started formulating her response when a second text appeared.

My phone tells me when you open my texts.

A twinge of panic hit her as her anger had already started to boil. She took another moment to compose her thoughts and responded with four texts sent slowly in succession for emphasis.

at my moms

She sent the first and waited a moment to follow with a 'thumbs up' emoji. After waiting a few seconds, she sent the 'middle finger' emoji, smiling at her mental image of Chase seeing it. To complete the run, she finished with a 'hysterically laughing' emoji just to soften the blow.

Still enjoying the moment of self-amusement and wondering if she left anything out, the image of

$$¯\_(ツ)_/¯$$

immediately appeared back from Chase followed by a 'heart' emoji. A breath later, the familiar ringtone she cut off during her drive filled the air.

"What!" she answered sharply.

"Hey, I just called to see how you are."

Callie rolled her eyes at his cavalier, remorseless opening.

"I'm at my mom's, Chase. I'm doing cartwheels. What do you think?"

Callie's sarcasm did not resonate with him.

"That's great, honey," he replied, trying to push happiness into the conversation. "I think you'll have a great weekend."

That remark pissed her off. Her initial instinct was to lay into him over the phone. But being within earshot of her mother and knowing it would not have any impact to change things, she decided to go for guilt.

"No, Chase, you're the one having the great weekend with friends, drinking, laughing, and golfing. I, on the other hand, am spending mine WITH MY MOTHER. We'll have lunch!"

Chase paused for a moment, trying to think of a believable spin to her comment.

"You like spending time with your mom."

He knew her tactic. To relinquish would be to admit he was wrong. He had to fight guilt with guilt.

"That's not what I meant, and you know it," she replied sternly. "You and I are married. We're supposed to be together... not fighting about being apart. I feel like... like we'll never have time together."

The line stayed silent. Callie pulled her phone from her ear to look at it to make sure they were still connected.

"It's my job, sweetie," came lightly back.

"This weekend is not about your job. It's playtime with your friends," Callie replied, irritated at his convenient bundling of the two.

"I've apologized for that already. Can we just move on?" he replied with some force to get his point across. "And a lot of this argument is about my job. It's not a nine-to-five office job that gets me home each and every night. That's why I get paid what I do."

Callie finally surrendered to the fact that nothing she could say would convince him that she missed them as a couple.

"How much longer do I have to wait until we get OUR time?" she asked, working hard to keep a calmer, quieter voice.

"I just can't stop."

"Chase... We have enough..."

Callie's voice was now shifting from disappointment to pleading, which she did not like and was not likely to get the response she wanted.

"Honey, it's never enough," he responded, confirming her expectation, and sinking her hopes. "This also isn't something we should debate on the phone at eleven o'clock at night. I'm tired. You're tired."

"You're just selfish and drunk!" she snapped back. "Just go back to drinking with your friends."

Callie's ability to stay calm dissolved as she immediately hung up and looked for the wine glass that sat empty on the end table beside her. Frustrated and angry, tears welled up as she struggled to keep them from rolling. She was not going to cry. But the reality became too much as her emotions and tears released into a quiet sobbing.

After a few moments, Callie regained her composure and dried her tears. She was now completely exhausted and stared hopelessly out at the lights off in the darkness. Their usual magic was not working.

Looking for a distraction, she reactivated her phone and began to close open apps. As she placed her finger on Sandy's Facebook, she saw it was still open to Jason's post. Looking for something that could divert her pain, she looked at his pictures again, first shaking her head in remembrance then with a light smile.

## 4

The rising morning sun filled the bedroom as Callie stood by the window overlooking the front lawn. Her Range Rover and the grounds were still wet from the overnight rain. The sky, however, looked promising for good weather.

Callie sat on the cushioned window seat to think. Her silk pajamas settled gently against her skin as she gazed out into the warm colors of the sunrise and landscape. A smile then came to her face as she stood to get her day started.

There was no sign of Carolyn being up as Callie quietly walked through the house and out the front door with her overnight bag. Molly trotted beside her, controlled by her leash. They both than settled into the Range Rover and drove away. A note for her mother was left on the kitchen counter to explain her unexpected absence.

Going to the beach to see a friend.

XXOO C

#

The rain began to fall again as Callie traveled on the interstate from Williamsburg toward the North Carolina coast. She did not have a plan for the day. She also was not sure if she would even make an effort to drive by Jason's cottage. Her initial vision reveled in the thought of doing something really crazy, like accidentally-on-purpose crossing paths with her former fiancé to truly see who he had become. Through all her thoughts of the possible things that could happen, what she discovered in herself was that the hurt and anger she had once felt from the events between them twenty-seven years ago were gone. As she thought more about a possible meeting with him, she started to get nervous about what was about to unfold.

It was not uncommon for Callie to think of Jason from time to time as life events happened. But she always knew that her feelings for him were rooted in memories and that her life with Chase and their kids was her purpose now. Still, she was becoming more and more drawn to see who Jason had become. She never considered her motives for wanting to see him as vengeance against her husband for his weekend choice. It was just curiosity and whether she had the courage to see her first love again.

The rain continued to fall lightly as she pulled into a convenience store and gas station. Her phone's GPS marked her close to his cottage. She parked on the lot's edge to relax and to ponder what was to come next. Facing toward the gas pumps, she anxiously watched as cars came and went. After a few minutes, her thoughts turned to words.

"Well? You're here. One mile from his house..." she muttered, appearing to come to a conclusion. "This is really stupid.... What are you doing here? No, this is dumb. Really dumb.... What the hell?"

Callie started the engine and put the car into drive. As she started to roll toward the exit nearest to where she had come from, an older, rag-topped Jeep Wrangler rolled past to the gas pumps. Instinct told her to stop. She watched as it pulled next to the pumps under a small driver-side awning.

Callie felt her stomach tighten and breathing become difficult as she watched a familiar face and frame emerge from the Jeep. He was older and gray. But he was also fit and well dressed for a beach dad who was driving an old Jeep. She smiled at the sight and focused on the image in front of her as he processed his credit card at the gas pump.

As Jason placed the hose to fill his gas tank, a large, brown head emerged out the back of the Jeep. Jason gave his furry companion a smile and a few head pats. Callie recognized the dog as a Chesapeake Bay Retriever who gratefully took the affection before disappearing under the cloth top. Callie became entranced by the dream-like scene unfolding in front of her. As Jason returned the hose to the gas pump, she regained consciousness to panic about her next step.

In all her thoughts driving down, Callie never thought through if and/or how she would approach him. One thing was certain; she could not just show up at his cottage. Their meeting had to look accidental. She did not know if he was either on his way out of town or heading back to his cottage for the day. And he was not dressed for the beach. So, this opportunity was her only option to be the site of an accidental run-in or to be lost.

Jason was back into the Jeep and started to pull away when he heard a loud slap against its side.

"Wait!"

That one word was all that Callie could muster as she bent over to catch her breath after sprinting to catch him.

The Jeep stopped abruptly as Jason looked back to see who had called out. After a moment of confusion, he focused on the familiar face covered by a hooded rain jacket, trying to catch her breath. A warm wash of emotion filled his body, resulting in a teary smile. As he stepped out of the Jeep, Callie walked closer to him, stopping a few feet away.

"Callie..." he whispered loud enough for her to hear while smiling at the image in front of him. "Hi... This can't be a coincidence."

Callie did not respond as she stood silently still peering out from under her hood. Jason stepped to her to give her a hug. Her firm grasp was real and familiar. It pulled down on his neck to show her feelings and always hurt. It was exactly what he remembered.

It was also no surprise to either of them that after twenty-seven years and all the hurt that had happened between them, an immediate, undeniable connection remained. As Jason let go, he pointed to a coffee shop across the street. Callie smiled and nodded, feeling both shame and excitement to be there with him.

# # #

The coffee shop was busy as patrons seeking both shelter from the rain and its unique social climate found their way in and stayed. Its rustic setting was comfortable and pleasant for sitting to pass the time. The baked goods were extensive, offering a variety of options from kid-friendly doughnuts to fine pastries for the parents and grandparents. As Callie took a seat at a table by the window facing the street, Jason collected and delivered two large ceramic cups that were steaming with the day's blend.

"I love places like this," Callie said, smiling while warming her hands against the mug.

Jason studied her face as he struggled to think of something clever to say.

"It's my favorite place to go... particularly when old girlfriends suddenly appear out of nowhere," he replied with a smirk.

"Hmmm. Happens to you a lot?"

Jason smiled while starting to shake his head *yes*. He then shook it *no*.

"No..." he confessed, trying, and losing his desire to hold back his smile. "You're the first."

Callie felt a sense of achievement in that declaration, causing her to sit up and lean toward him.

"I hope I'm not just thought of as an old girlfriend," she inquired, eager to hear a confirming response.

"No doubt about that," he answered without hesitation.

Callie felt elevated. She smiled and took a pull of coffee. Jason watched her expressions with interest, waiting for a like compliment from her that did not come. The conversation stalled as each thought through what they could say without saying too much.

"Will your dog be OK in your car?" he asked, looking for something innocuous. "Are those leather seats cooled? Or are they just heated?"

The absurdity of the question amused Callie as she looked to see Molly steaming the windshield while watching her every move. Was that the best he could come up with after twenty-seven years apart? She paused to answer, knowing that would make him more anxious.

"She'll be fine," she answered, working hard to not show any expression of amusement. "She rides with me all the time. What about yours? Is his tetanus up to date?"

Jason savored the jab. Mrs. Range Rover was poking fun at his Jeep.

"He's a HER and she's fine. She'll stay put," he responded. "Tetanus? That's good."

"Does SHE eat smaller dogs?" Callie immediately responded to keep it going.

"No," he replied adamantly. "At least... well, how small are we talking about?"

Jason sat back in his chair, enjoying Callie's surprised look to his reply. He took a pull from his mug as she digested the question. Her initial thoughts were concern until she noted the grin on his face that showed he was joking. Callie did not like that he could still push her buttons. She sat back in her chair and just peered at him curiously over her mug. And now that she was off balance, Jason could not resist following up with another question.

"So... I'm surprised to just run into you here. Just driving through?"

Jason maintained a stoic look, knowing full well the question presented an awkward situation for her. Callie replied without thinking because she felt it was easy to explain.

"I suppose," she answered. "I had an open weekend. I was visiting my mom and—"

"Your mom lives in Williamsburg," Jason interrupted.

Callie felt the sensation of being trapped. She quickly ran through some responses. None made any sense.

"Yes. My parents... I guess... it's just Mom now lives in—"

"Williamsburg." Jason smiled, not resisting the opportunity to interject again. "Two hours away. I googled her house. Very nice... with a view of the James River."

Callie smirked and shook her head in disbelief.

"Oh, come on," he confessed. "Like you never googled my address."

"I didn't have to," she replied. "You lived in your childhood neighborhood, down the hill and across the street from mine."

Jason knew he was caught through his Google explanation and decided not to ask how she knew where he still lived there. He had been creeping on his former fiancée's parents' home in Williamsburg well after they ended their relationship. It was no surprise that she either did the same or knew from shared friends where he lived.

"Yes, I suppose you didn't have to look," he replied. "Not too exciting."

"Kinda sad if you ask me," she said as she noted a little hurt appear in his face.

Callie could not resist making the jab without thinking. But afterward, she felt that she should have.

"I suppose," Jason admitted, seeing an opportunity to tee up his next clever poke. "It's certainly not DC."

Surprised, Callie gave him a puzzled look.

"I googled your house too," he smiled, then paused to receive only a blank stare. "Fancy."

Callie shook her head in disbelief, trying to process why Jason would find her address then google her home in Great Falls decades after their split. Jason stayed silent as she processed her thoughts. He was now looking for an opportunity to stop the friendly jabs back and forth that were starting to get out of hand.

"I was sorry to hear about your dad," he said to break the silence, and to change the subject. "He was a wonderful man."

"I got your letter," she responded quietly, surprised by the drastic shift of topic.

"That's good. I wasn't sure. You didn't respond."

Jason's face softened to express the sadness he felt. That Callie was across the table made the conversation more difficult.

"Did you really expect me to write you back?" she asked. "To be honest, it kinda pissed me off."

Jason took a moment to think through what he had long suspected.

"I was afraid of that. I had no right to write you. But, your dad, man... he could've, should've for that matter, crushed me after you and I split. He certainly had the right to do it. But he didn't. I'm not so sure I'd be that gracious if anything close to that happened to one of my girls."

Callie felt a twinge of anger as she listened to his confession. She never suspected that Jason held either any regret or remorse about their split.

"Well, don't think for a moment that thought didn't cross his mind," she answered, blinded by her new feelings. "Or that I would have stopped him."

Callie's expression showed a seriousness that concerned him. But it evaporated as she continued to look at his face full of new lines and wrinkles, not part of her past images of him.

"Fact is, though, he really liked you," she added. "And he loved us."

Jason found a refreshing comfort in her comment. A few months after their separation, he crossed paths with Callie's parents while out dining. Caught in a situation where each saw the other, Callie's dad invited him over to their table for a brief, very friendly discussion. Jason was so moved by the event that he wrote them a thank-you note for being so gracious. Callie's comment now explained their treatment of him after the split.

"We were a good-looking couple," he said in reflection. "You know what my mother's first comment was after our split? 'You would've had beautiful children'.... 'You would've had beautiful children.'"

Jason repeated the comment, chuckling at the memory.

"She was right, ya know," Callie replied without hesitation.

"Only if they took after their mother," he added with a toast of his mug. "Do you remember the night we had dinner with your whole family? Oh my God, that was intimidating."

Callie's face lit with the remembrance as Jason leaned in.

"How could I ever forget it?" she answered, smiling to the image that appeared in her head.

Both Callie and Jason could see the same picture of the formally set table that included Callie's two sisters and her parents at the table heads.

"Your dad was going through all your very Catholic names. Mary Patricia, Mary Margaret and you, young Callie, Mary Calista. Throwing the heavy-duty Catholic directly at the poor infidel Protestant trying to marry into the family."

"I was waiting for you to run," she laughed. "But that's when you said... let me get this right... 'wasn't it great that your initials were J.C.?' Very gutsy."

Callie's smug imitation of Jason's comment was perfect. Both laughed at the memory.

"It just came out. Could've ended it all right there."

"Nope. He loved it," she said. "You held your own. He respected that."

Callie's face quickly turned blank with the remembrance. The sadness of losing her dad, although almost a decade ago, was still painful. It reminded Jason of one comment her father made to him in private just after announcing their engagement.

You know, you got the best one.

Jason needed to console her through these memories.

"He got his point across. I miss him," he said, looking to segue to a happier subject.

"I do too," she whispered back.

Their conversation was beginning to stall when Callie looked out to her car again for signs of Molly, who continued to keep a watchful eye on her through the front windshield. As she collected herself from her emotions, a faint smile appeared her face.

"You look good! Seem to be in a good place here. Happy?"

Jason half heard her question. He was still caught in the realization that she was across the table from him.

"For now. I suppose," he replied with an uncertain smile. "It's nice to see you."

With that statement, Callie immediately felt a need to reevaluate her situation. She was at the beach across the table from her former fiancé while her husband golfed thinking she was two hours away from there having lunch with her mother. The attraction from twenty-seven years ago that led to her accepting Jason's marriage proposal was reemerging. Feelings that could not resurface now. They were also the same feelings that called her to the beach to see him when things were difficult with her husband. She needed a break from their conversation to reassess if this time together needed to end. She found one.

"Look. The rain has stopped. Do you have time to show me your beach?"

Jason's eyes lit at the suggestion. It was obvious to Callie that he was not having the same internal struggles as she was. But why would he? He was divorced and single with no cares. That led her to ponder whether or not the time he was giving her now was genuine or just a rude attempt to conquer her again. Thinking this made her mad at herself, not only for thinking badly of him, but also for putting herself into a situation where it could happen.

"I'm just over a mile from here," he answered, pulling her attention back. "I'd love to show you my place."

## 5

Callie followed behind the Jeep as it navigated through the narrow, sand-lined streets. Jason was driving annoyingly slow to ensure she didn't get lost behind him. But Callie's nerves had her wishing he would just step on it like she remembered when she used to complain about him driving too fast.

The houses along the shoreline were a mix of old and new. The older homes were more modest single-floor cottages. The newer houses were grander, multi-floor monstrosities with decks and crows-nest features projecting out in all directions. If Callie had to choose a house for her family, she knew Chase would only want the newer, bigger, and more elaborate beach house. The smaller cottage just was not 'him'. She had already seen pictures of Jason's cottage and did not expect to be wowed. She was not disappointed.

The two cars pulled off the beach road onto the parking pad under Jason's cottage. The parking spaces sat next to each other. Some piles of building materials were stacked neatly and out of the way. Zoe jumped out of the Jeep with Jason. Off-lead, she immediately headed over to greet their new guests. Callie had Molly on a leash, who immediately cowered to Zoe's advances and sniffs. Jason grabbed Zoe's collar as Callie took her first look around to form her first impression.

"Well, it's not much now," he stated, almost apologetically, "but it's home."

Callie, concerned for Molly, did not know what to say.

"A work in progress…. It's… you," was all she said while she addressed her dog's fear. It sounded more complimentary in her head than when verbalized.

Jason gave her a puzzled look as he started to pull his exuberant dog away from her interest.

"I don't quite know how to take that…"

He then released Zoe toward the cottage stairs.

"Zoe. Go away."

Zoe ran up the stairs and disappeared up onto the elevated walkway. She then quickly returned to the top of the stairs, barking for her new friend to join her.

"You can let her go," Jason said, pointing to the stairs. "No one will be out there. I think the walkway is gated."

Callie hesitantly unclipped Molly who took off after Zoe. Jason and Callie then looked at each other with like surprise.

"We should probably follow them," they said in unison.

Without hesitation, they both headed for the stairs that led to up to the house and to the beach. They laughed as they started to climb the stairs like two children racing. Jason let Callie go ahead of him and touched her back to guide her as she passed by. Instinctively, he pulled his hand back as she looked back over her shoulder. She smiled at his discomfort for the simple touch. His reaction had just erased her concerns regarding his thoughts and interests for their time together.

As Callie reached the walkway, Jason's view of the ocean emerged. The cottage sat between two large, recently constructed beach homes that overshadowed his. But every house and cottage sat the same distance back from the dune. Looking left and right, Callie noted that the new, bigger homes all had pools in the space between the house and the dune. The cottages, however, tended to only have sand yards that hosted their elevated walkways to their pool, which was the ocean.

As they reached the end of the walkway, Callie noticed the built-in sitting area that overlooked the water. She looked for and found Molly and Zoe running circles around each other near the foot of Jason's stairs. Callie was amused by the immediate friendship Molly had established with Zoe. It also intrigued her that no one was out on the sand on a warm Saturday October afternoon.

"See, all to ourselves," Jason remarked, as he pointed out over the expansive beach. "Let's go for a walk."

Callie relished the feel of the sand as it packed down beneath her feet and into her toes when she stepped off the stairs. As they walked, a perfect trail of foot impressions recorded their steps. The dogs ran ahead while continuing to circle around each other. The setting seemed perfect as neither she nor Jason noticed the threatening skies blowing onshore. Their thoughts were on each other as they worked through the newness of their situation and what to talk about next. After a brief conversation about the houses and the beach, another awkward silence came between them.

"For two people who haven't seen each other in over two decades, we certainly ran out of stuff to talk about really fast," Jason said to break the silence as he reached for a shell in the sand.

"Just picking up where we left off," she answered, eager to see his reaction.

Bent over, Jason stopped cold to laugh at the sharpness of the jab.

"Oh my God. Did you really just say that?" He chuckled as he stood and handed her the shell.

Callie smiled as she examined what he found, then tossed it away.

"Oh, come on," she answered. "Just a little smack to get the conversation going."

Although her tone was playful, Callie was putting Jason on notice that her presence there was not insinuating anything to include any forgiveness of past events.

"Smack? Really?"

Callie bumped him playfully as thunder rumbled above and the rain restarted with a sudden fury. Jason grabbed her hand as they began their run for shelter. The dogs, led by Zoe, reached the stairs first. All four of them finished their dash across the walkway to the house together. Covered only by a wood frame pergola, the rain continued to soak them as Jason struggled to open the sliding door. He did his best to shield Callie while sidestepping the two dogs who pressed to the glass at his feet. As the door opened to the dryness inside, the four water-soaked runners entered and created slippery footing on the wood floor. When Jason looked to help Callie, they started to laugh as they both frantically reached to grab their dogs.

Jason threw Callie a towel for Molly from a basket by the door as Zoe shook, spraying him, the floor, and the door with water and wet sand. Callie laughed harder as he shielded himself from the spray, then slipped to his bum while trying to maintain control of his dog. Molly then shook next to Callie, which created the same reaction from Jason as she squirmed to both maintain her footing and to shield herself from the spray as she smothered Molly with the towel. As Jason stood, he grabbed another towel to cover Zoe who then danced beneath it. Zoe loved the feel of towel over her head. As the commotion ended, both Jason and Callie looked at each other in shared exasperation for what had just happened.

"I'm sorry. The sand… the wet," Callie apologized, while still addressing Molly's soaked coat.

"Don't worry. It's not the first time. It'll all sweep up," Jason responded.

"Still, it's going to be a mess."

Callie started to look around while finishing Molly's towel-off. It was her first look into Jason's life and taste for furnishings at his bachelor pad. The outside did not indicate that any great care had been taken to furnish the inside. But that impression was wrong. Although skewed heavily male with too much leather and dark colors for a beach cottage, the decor was complete and well-appointed with quality art uncommon to properties she had seen even in the high-rent communities of Nantucket.

"The outside doesn't represent the inside," she remarked without thinking.

Jason took the towel back from her, noticing her attention had shifted from drying Molly to surveying his home.

"You're soaked," he replied, leaving her comment to hang. "Let me get you something to change into."

"I have a change of clothes in the car," she responded.

The implication of her comment did not resonate with her until she noticed the surprised look on his face.

"I AM visiting my mother for the weekend," she added matter-of-factly with a tinge smugness. "I brought clothes."

Jason relaxed as Callie smiled at the mixed message in her comment. Visiting her mother was already tossed aside at the coffee shop when she explained how she found him at the beach.

"Great!" he responded. "Let me go get them for you. You can take a shower if you want to warm up."

Surprised by the otherwise logical offer to someone rain-soaked and likely cold, Callie did not respond. The thought of her being naked in his home seemed wrong. But the reality was that she was soaked and freezing. A hot shower followed by clean, dry clothes was the solution. For a moment, a flash of him joining her in the shower appeared in her head, then quickly flickered out. She reached into her pocket and tossed him the keys to her car.

"I'll be a good boy. I promise," Jason said snidely, having had the same image in his head. "Towels are right there. I'll put your bag in the guest room across from the bathroom."

Callie smiled cautiously at his comment and watched him leave. The dogs tried to follow but were stopped as the door closed on them.

# # #

The storm eased as Jason descended the stairs to the parking area. Protected by the structure above them, both cars and all the neatly stacked construction materials were dry. As Jason approached Callie's car, the faint sound of the door unlocking along with the flashers blinking and interior lights illuminating showed that he could access the car for her bag. As he opened the back-passenger door, he heard the water turn on, indicating that Callie was undressing above him.

The Range Rover's interior permeated a rich, new car smell with a hint of perfume he recognized. He washed his hand over the leather seats and smiled at its richness.

"I'm glad you got this," he mumbled quietly to himself as he continued to survey the interior of her car. He grabbed her rolling suitcase, noting its high-end luster and happy to see it had wheels.

The shower stopped as Jason started down the short hallway from the living room to the sleeping area. His guest room sat opposite the bathroom door, which created a tight space as the three bedroom doors all presented to the hallway near each other. The third bedroom was the first to appear on the left when walking from the living room. Jason put Callie's bag down and continued into his bedroom to change out of his still-wet shorts and shirt.

As he popped his head through his new, dry t-shirt, Callie appeared from the bathroom wrapped in a towel. She stopped briefly to lock eyes with him, smiled, then rolled her bag into the guest room. The door closed behind her.

# # #

Sun and blue skies radiated abundant as Callie emerged through the sliding door wearing a white William and Mary t-shirt and street shorts. As with a lot of coastal storms, the bad weather disappeared as quickly as it arrived.

Callie's look was soft and casual with her hair brushed-back in a slick style that illuminated her face. Jason and the dogs were at the end of the walkway. The gate to the beach was closed to keep Molly and Zoe on the platformed surface. To her surprise, the two dogs were still getting to know each other with some soft rough housing that would ordinarily have made her nervous. Jason had his back to her as he surveyed the ocean. He turned as the dogs diverted their attention from each other to Callie as she approached.

"That felt great. You going to shower?" she asked as she walked up beside him.

Her dress and demeanor showed a genuine comfort in being there. She was barefoot, which was a welcome sign that she was going to stay for a while, maybe even for dinner, before she had to head back to Williamsburg.

"I'll shower later," he responded. "The hot water needs to recover."

"I only took a short shower."

"I know. I didn't mean to insinuate that you took an excessive shower," he said, recalling her history of soaking baths and showers when they were together. "That's just one of the changes yet to make. Old tank. Good for just me. Not so good with guests."

Jason's embarrassment amused Callie. His unwavering stare at her in her casual attire and hair was welcoming and felt natural.

"I have to confess," Callie remarked. "I snooped a little.... You have very good taste for a man and really nice art for a beach house.... I even recognized a few pieces."

Jason smiled at the comment. Several pieces displayed prominently in the cottage were buys he and Callie had made while dating. None of the pieces were either expensive or collector quality. It was just art that they both appreciated while out on adventures together.

"You should recognize quite a few," he replied without hesitation. "You and I bought them together."

"And you kept them."

"I kept a lot of things," Jason replied. "But in my office, mostly. My wife knew some of the history. So, it was either my office or boxes.... auction or the dump, if she had her way."

Callie smiled at the mental image. Jason felt a twinge of sadness flow through him as he watched her reaction, realizing what they had lost over the last twenty-seven years. He sniffed to keep his emotions hidden. She was there now, with him, for who knows how long and why. His goal was not to let anything spoil that. His need was to move on to a more positive topic.

"It's amazing to me how fast the weather changes here," he remarked.

The weather was always a good topic for Jason when conversations needed to be redirected. Callie, however, thought his statement was an odd, given their current situation.

"Ya know... I don't recall you being much of a beach person," she mused, knowing it to be both true and counter to his current living situation. "Something about the salt, the sand, and—"

"The sun." Jason completed, as if he had practiced for hours. "If not for those, I'd like the beach. My ex was the beach fanatic; so, my kids love the beach. I came around. I bought this place for them, for us."

"Still sail?" she asked.

"No," he answered, embarrassed by the confession. "Not yet. But that is something I want to do again."

"Work?" she added. "I mean, you can't live here and be close to an office."

"Consult," he replied, puzzled by the add-on to the question. "I sold my company last year. It was easiest for settling out the divorce and the offer was generous."

"So, retired at fifty-five?"

"I don't think so," he replied, seeming to ponder some things. "We'll see."

Jason held an uncertain look as he peered out over the water. Callie watched as his eyes glossed over.

"And there he goes," she said, shaking her head at the one quality he had that used to infuriate her more than any other.

"What's that?" he replied, oblivious to what just happened.

"We were talking, and you just disappeared into your own head mid-conversation."

Jason smiled at the accusation. He knew it to be true. Callie made no secret that his habit of leaving conversations hanging while internalizing various thoughts was annoying to her. He also found it warming that she not only still had no patience for it, but that she also did not hesitate to say anything about it.

"My ex, Stephanie, used to find that annoying too."

"I get that, and I know who Stephanie is," Callie replied, trying to hold a serious look while savoring his discomfort.

Jason motioned to Callie to sit on the bench that overlooked the water. The bench was not only Jason's solitude spot up and away from the grit and commotion of the beach, it was also his perch to watch everything that happened on the sand and in the water.

As a new resident living alone, the bench was his place to enjoy the scents, sounds, and cleanliness of the ocean while not putting himself between families who rented the homes to his left and to his right. It was his observation deck for watching the world. He placed a towel down on the moist wooden surface. He then sat next to her as he watched a family wade into the water.

"This is my favorite time of day," he said, with his eyes focused out over the water. "The air is warm. The sun is at your back. Young families with kids—that aren't mine—are on the beach... but I have to say, it's much better in the summer."

"We have friends that come here. Or at least, somewhere on the Outer Banks,"

Jason's focus on a family in the water intrigued Callie. His attention was no less intense than a new father watching his first child wade in unsupervised.

"It's a big place with lots of DC folks here," he replied with what sounded like an auto-response.

Callie sat for a moment watching him study the family in the surf. His attention was completely on them and not on anything she was saying.

"Are you living here year-round?" she asked, trying to pull him back.

His head cocked to the side as he squinted. That was his way of tuning back into what was in front of him rather than off in some distant field of thought.

"That's actually a good question," he answered. "I haven't thought that far out."

His face lit up as he focused back on Callie and her very pertinent question. It was a reality he had thought of many times but never made either a final decision or plan to solve.

As they both thought about the absurdness of Jason's lack of planning, a woman's yell pulled them both back to the present. When they looked to see why, adults from nearby families and beach walkers were running toward her. Jason abruptly stood to see what caused the outcry.

Out in the surf, a young girl was stumbling through the incoming waves as the force and tumble of the water knocked her off balance as each wave passed. Two dads had worked their way out into the surf to reach her. Once secured, the three slowly made their way to shore where the girl collapsed on the sand, sobbing. The adults immediately placed towels around her for warmth, as a woman, who appeared to be her mother, comforted her.

It did not surprise Callie that Jason jumped up and was attentive to what was happening. It was his nature to jump in if needed, when needed. But now that the girl was safe, she wondered why he stayed so focused on the scene.

"Everything OK?" she asked.

Jason remained silent, watching the scene cool down. The young girl was back on her feet and walking toward the dune and their beach house.

"Looks like it," he responded. "The rip currents here can be nasty. Not real smart to swim when tide's going out, particularly on stormy days. They must be renters."

Callie raised her eyebrows to his comment, making sure he saw it as he turned to look at her. Mr. 'I don't like the beach' was now a professional since buying his own cottage less than a year earlier.

Jason saw the humor in his comment but was not going to give her the satisfaction of appearing embarrassed. He kept his serious face intact, hoping she would not take the opportunity to dig in further.

"Um, hmm," was all Callie could muster as he came back into their conversation. "Now, about this winter. It's October. You might want to think about that. This place will be dead."

Jason thought for a moment.

"Well, it's just me and Zoe. I'll definitely stay here through Thanksgiving. All the kids have committed to come. They'll definitely go to her for Christmas. So, I guess the question after that is sun or snow?"

Callie smiled. "I'd go sun."

Jason knew that would be her position. He knew she hated the cold and particularly despised the snow. He remembered that from their life conversations while dating and during the Cleveland and DC winters they shared. Callie was an adventurer and would have gone anywhere warm. Jason was a skier, but not a person who liked cold weather at any other time. They were on the same track to find a life destination somewhere warmer when they were engaged.

"Kinda thinking that too," he responded, excited, as if they both had decided to head off to the tropics together. "My kids will come visit me there... Maybe you can visit me too?"

The remark just added itself to the end of his comment and fell flat. The slip had to be excused as one. But, in his heart, Callie visiting sometime during the winter would be a continuation of the dream he was living now. Her non-response of not even a smile gave him hope. As the invitation continued to hang in the air unanswered, a boisterous conversation of young parents walking toward them on the beach arrived before they did.

The women appeared first. Each one was wearing a beach cover of different design and size. Callie noted their shapes as they came closer. Jason waved to Rebecca, who smiled and enthusiastically waved back. Callie did not miss Rebecca for her perfectly tan, lean, and fit figure as she walked over to the foot of the stairs. She also felt a tinge of jealousy as Rebecca comfortably stepped on the stair and maintained an eye-lock on Jason. She also felt slightly ashamed that her initial thought was *'of course it's her, and not one of the rounder ones'.* But Jason did not belong to Callie. And, maybe, this woman did.

"Hey, Jason," Rebecca called out. "Happy hour on the beach later."

Beach happy hours were the norm for Callie's family and friends on Nantucket. So, there was no surprise for the suggestion, even in mid-October. In fact, the mid-October North Carolina air felt like Nantucket in August. What Callie did find amusing was that Rebecca's invitation was more of a statement than a question. Jason did not appear to mind as he was quick to confirm, perhaps thinking Callie would be on her way back to Williamsburg by then.

"Wouldn't miss it," he answered, not seeking details.

Callie's amusement of the exchange was pasted on her face as he turned to look at her. It surprised him that she was so tuned in and noted a tinge of 'something' in her expression.

"New friends," he said, trying not to laugh.

"New HOT friend," Callie replied, with a hint of accusation.

"They're all owners. ALL MARRIED and in for the weekend," he answered as he sat back down next to her. "They actually thought I was going to level this place and build a McMansion like these others."

"That was your original plan, wasn't it?"

Callie's tone made her question more of a statement of what she knew to be true.

No... Ok, well maybe... but small," he answered. "That was until I realized I'd lose this year to construction... and the cottage size fit me better. They do NOT know that so..."

"Your secret is safe with me," Callie interjected to give him comfort that she would not share his initial intent.

Jason nodded to confirm her promise. There was a seriousness in her expression that assured him that she was on his side. He took a moment to think through what that meant and where it was possibly heading. All the signals were crossing.

"Why don't you sit and enjoy this. I'm going to take a shower and clean up."

Jason needed time to sort out what had just happened and was happening. He knew he was facing a lukewarm shower, at best. But that, or colder, just may be right to give him a moment to collect his thoughts for some clarity.

"Should I change?" Callie asked, wondering about how she was dressed and implying that she would be joining him in the shower.

"No. You look great," he smiled while admiring her casual look. "Just enjoy this. I'll be right back."

Jason turned to walk the one-hundred-foot wooden walkway back to the cottage. Zoe followed as she always did, which drew Molly along with them. After entering the house, Jason closed the sliding glass door, leaving the dogs outside. They both watched, panting and fogging both the glass and their vision, to see if Jason went inside to get food. As he disappeared down the hallway, their excitement vanished as they realized his mission was not food oriented. When the dogs returned to Callie, they found her seated to face back toward the afternoon sun shining over the back of the cottages. Her eyes were closed to enjoy the warmth on her face as she savored the smells and sounds of the ocean around her.

## 6

There was a light onshore breeze blowing toward the low-hanging setting sun as Jason and Callie walked from his stairs to the party. Music was playing from a few well-positioned wireless JBL speakers as the adult chatter and laughter added color. Callie looked toward Jason as they stepped together, getting closer and closer to the party. He smiled and grabbed her hand to comfort her. But the touch that was meant for comfort sent a wave of panic through her being. The setting was surreal. On any other day, this would be in Nantucket, with Chase walking beside her. The partygoers would be familiar friends rather than a group of strangers eager to see who Jason had tagging along.

Callie noted the familiar face from the beach group they had seen earlier who had invited Jason to the party. She was a striking, strawberry-blond, mid-forties woman with soft Southern features and voice. As they approached, she was the first to step forward to greet them.

"Heyyyy, glad you could make it," she said in an excited tone.

Jason gave her a hug while Callie watched, standing helplessly behind him. He then stepped back to survey the party for who was there.

"Ya know, I prefer these every night instead of just on the weekends," he said jokingly while standing protectively in front of Callie.

"Well, Jay-son, some of us still have kids in school," the woman responded in a sharp-witted tone while turning her attention and reaching her hand out to Callie.

"Heyyy, I'm Rebecca."

"Callie," was the only response Callie could muster, feeling a bit intimidated and out of her depth.

Rebecca Newsome was a fourth-generation resident who lived in Richmond, Virginia. A Southern Belle in presentation and a physician by profession, Rebecca was the first resident to greet Jason when he appeared in the late spring. She was also his initial introduction to the close-knit group of owners who were very conservation oriented with specific goals to protect the small cottages from being bulldozed for bigger homes.

Jason's need for Callie to keep his secret that he considered tearing down the cottage was because over the course of the summer he openly denied having ever had any plan to replace his cottage with a newer house. That denial soon became the truth as he grew to love the materials, simplicity, and history of the beach cottages that still remained.

"Nice to meet you, Callie," Rebecca replied with a big welcoming smile. "You in for the weekend?"

Callie was puzzled on how to reply. Her answer would have implications. She held a blank stare for a few seconds which, to her, seemed much longer.

"Good question," she finally said, feeling some relief. "I don't know…"

Jason started to realize Callie's dilemma. And, as amusing as it was to watch her squirm, he knew he had to jump in to give her a respectable out.

"Callie's an old friend from Cleveland," he added, trying to redirect the conversation.

Rebecca smiled, sensing there was something more to their story.

"Well, we're glad you're here," she said while looking back and forth between them. "We're getting a special spot for you Clevelanders because of this guy."

Callie felt some relief as she watched Rebecca put her hand on Jason's shoulder. The group appeared to be genuine, unlike her ultra-judging cluster of social-climbing friends back in the DC area. Although she had many friends she could trust with her deepest secrets, Callie had to be careful when talking to anyone about anything during formal and informal social gatherings. There was something different about Rebecca that instilled an immediate trust.

"Just know..." Rebecca declared with a smile and raise of her glass, "you probably won't be legal to drive anywhere after this social."

Rebecca's forewarning of the drinking was on target. The crowd became livelier as time and spirits passed. Callie met many long-time owners and was surprised to have genuine conversations about relatively nothing with each of them. Through the evening, she became quite good at directing conversations to and away from specific topics. As she did, she realized that she was using the same tactics Chase would use on her when either wanting or not wanting to talk about certain things.

As she finished her last conversation, Jason touched her on the shoulder to say he was going to help the men move something on the beach and that he would be right back. Callie smiled and encouraged him to run off with the boys to do their thing. She was comfortable in this new setting and turned her attention to the water as he walked off. She took a few steps away from the group to collect her thoughts.

"I don't believe we've met," came from behind her in an exaggerated, syrup-thick Southern accent.

Callie turned on her smile as she turned to greet the voice that was seeking her attention. As she paired the face with the voice, she was intimidated by the presence of Celeste Regus whose trainer-fit body and bronze complexion showed well through the thin veil of a beach cover she was wearing. Celeste was garnished in full, tastefully done makeup and well-presented casual hair. Callie immediately felt a sense of competitive conflict.

"I'm Callie. I'm here with—"

"Jason," Celeste finished, leading Callie to wonder if finishing other people's sentences was a beach thing on the Outer Banks.

Callie could sense that Celeste was unhappy to see her there. Her body language was positioned to intimidate, which she found annoying. She saw it all the time in social settings in DC. She was puzzled to see it at a casual beach party in North Carolina.

"I'm Celeste," she added, as she reached out her hand and presented a firm shake. "I didn't know that Jason was seeing anyone. It's nice to meet you."

Celeste was studying Callie for who she was and what she presented. Callie correctly sensed that Celeste had an interest in Jason that was either not happening or not happening to what Celeste wanted. Celeste's first impression was that Callie was a significant threat. Callie saw humor in the situation and decided to play along.

"We're not seeing each other now," Callie answered, as she watched Celeste's eyes zero in on her. "Jason and I were engaged long ago and we just ran into each other today. Funny, isn't it?"

Callie watched Celeste process the information.

"My name's Callie," she repeated awkwardly, realizing she had introduced herself already.

"Nice to meet you. Callie... is it?" Celeste answered while deepening her Southern drawl. "We're happy to have you here this evening."

Celeste's smile was fake and presented like a dog's growl without the noise. Callie knew that she had struck a nerve, which was fun in just having another woman jealous of her. The fact that it could cause Jason some pain later was just a little more perverse joy as retaliation for his past actions.

"Having a good time?" brought Callie back into real time as Rebecca approached from behind.

Celeste smiled with a look of dissatisfaction and took Rebecca's approach as her cue to leave. There was something about Callie that told Celeste that her opportunities for Jason were over. Not unfamiliar with having summer relationships end, Celeste just turned and walked away as Callie and Rebecca giggled at her rudeness.

"Having a good time?" Rebecca asked again, still amused by Celeste's departure.

"Yes... I am. This is great," Callie answered, looking for the right thing to say to the woman who she thought caught Jason's fancy. "This is my first time here. We usually go to Nantucket."

Rebecca walked closer and smiled at Callie's compliment while trying to figure out if it was genuine, or just a dig on their little, lesser known, and less appreciated spot of sand on the ocean.

"I hear Nantucket's nice too," she replied quickly to keep things civil. "I've been coming here all my life. Now my husband and I bring our kids... and dogs. It's the perfect place."

Callie nodded in appreciation, warming Rebecca's impression of her.

"It is, isn't it?" Callie answered while looking around the shoreline. "Jason seems to like it here. He seems at peace."

Rebecca's amusement from the comment puzzled Callie. Jason's apparent happiness and authentic group of friends proved to Rebecca that her observation was right about Callie. But she could not figure out what she was missing. She looked around to ensure that no one was in earshot before she started to speak in a quieter voice.

"He does now. But he was a mess... and a lot heavier, when he first arrived," Rebecca started as she continued to look around. "It was interesting, and kinda funny, to watch him. He kept to himself. That cottage was his project. But he also did the usual guy things. He ran a little on the beach. Then he biked. Had the outfit and everything... that didn't last too long. Then, he got into swimming towards the end of July... He swims a lot."

It surprised Callie to hear about Jason's evolution over the summer months. Her memory of him was as a moderate weekend warrior athlete who would bike, hike, and ski to the seasons. She remembered his build as fit but not cut. However, that was long ago when a good diet and regular exercise was not as necessary as it was now. Some of the pictures of him on Facebook showed significantly more pounds than he should have carried. Her hope then was that it was probably just a bad camera angle. But maybe he did let himself go during the marriage. A thought she was now connecting to Chase, whose waistline had been expanding a lot over the past ten years.

"I thought his nice shape was from working on the cottage," Callie replied.

Rebecca responded with a smile, finding a funny naivete in her comment.

"Oh no, he has contractors doing the heavy lifting there. Ya know, we expected him to level it. We know that was his original plan. He thinks we don't. But we do."

Callie found irony in the trust that both sides were giving her, despite neither really knowing her.

"Your secret's safe with me," she whispered, while playfully leaning toward her and doing her best not to smile.

Rebecca appreciated Callie's promise to keep her slip of the tongue between them. She was careful not to share what she suspected Jason originally wanted to do, fearful that he would either be offended or take it as their permission to move forward with his original plan to level the cottage. As Callie took a sip of drink, Rebecca's face gained a renewed focus as if studying her.

"He's a really good person," Rebecca declared, in a deliberate tone.

"Always has been," Callie replied quickly, trying her best to hold her ground and not push back on the insinuation that she was there for any other reason than to just see him.

Rebecca continued to study Callie as she watched her nervously take another sip of her drink.

"He has four daughters. Can you imagine?"

Rebecca waited to see Callie's response for shock. If Callie was really an old friend, she would know about his kids. She did not blink. She was real.

"I've only met the youngest," Rebecca added. "The others haven't shown up yet. That youngest is sweet. But she's a handful."

"I get it," Callie answered as she re-situated from her last sip of cocktail. "I was the third of three girls. I told him if my parents were a forest, my oldest sister Patty cleared the trees so my other sister Maggie could pave the lot that I got to drive all over... I can't imagine four girls. I only have three kids, and only one daughter, and that's enough."

A smile appeared on Rebecca's face that eased the tension created by trying to figure out who Callie was to Jason.

"I've heard that saying. Jason says that's his life to a *T*. Now, I know the source," she said, while adding an appreciative toast of her cup.

"That's me," Callie answered, taking a sip to buy a moment.

"Do you see him often?"

The question and its timing caused Callie to inhale quickly, drawing her drink down her windpipe. She coughed, then stuttered through her response.

"No... Sorry..." Callie forced out as she regained her breath. "I haven't seen him in almost twenty-seven years."

"Wow, that's amazing," Rebecca replied with slight surprise. "You look so comfortable together."

Callie debated how much to share. Was Rebecca trustworthy? She had just shared her deepest Jason secret with her. She might as well fill in the rest with the backstory.

"We were a couple once... actually engaged... for a while... then... well, when that didn't happen, he went his way and I moved to DC, got married and raised my family."

As Callie finished their history, she realized that her cup was in her left hand, front and center to Rebecca's line of sight.

"So, you're married?" Rebecca asked, surprised by the confession, and focused on the rings on Callie's wedding finger.

The question came as an embarrassing surprise to Callie. She traveled to the beach, not having thought through much of anything. Her original thought was to, maybe, see him from a distance for fun, then turn around and go back to her mom's. But that changed when she chased him down at the gas station. And it now was even deeper as she was being presented and was socializing with his friends as either his girl interest or girlfriend. She had no scripted position responses to rattle off, which is something she did not learn from Chase.

"Me? No. I mean. Yes. I am," Callie finally surrendered, knowing she was caught. "My husband is on a golf weekend with his buddies. So, I thought, why not go to the beach?"

The attempt at humor did not appear to resonate with Rebecca. Her look of surprise and some disapproval was apparent. Callie had to find a path out of the discussion for her to save face and for Jason not to look like a wife-stealing cad.

"I'm just down here to visit my mother in Williamsburg. Thought I'd stop by... for a vis... it."

Rebecca said nothing as Callie continued trying to explain her path to getting there. Through the silence, Callie knew the entire scenario she was painting was not believable. Her presence with Jason screamed 'affair' now that Rebecca knew she was married.

"I just assumed you were a new girl interest, which I was happy to see," Rebecca interjected, to lighten the mood. "He really looks happy with you. And he hasn't had anyone here on his arm until, well, now. And there's been interest from the beach community. But they're all mostly married, just like you. Celeste excluded, of course."

Rebecca was sensitive to the awkwardness that Callie had just waded into. She felt compassion for her, knowing that there had to be a reason for Callie to make her way from Williamsburg to the beach to find Jason. Her concern, however, was whether that reason was healthy for either of them.

"I have to be honest; this visit is a surprise to me too," Callie added. "Yesterday I was yelling at my husband for taking a golf trip and—"

"Now you're here," Rebecca blurted out. An immediate look of regret hit her face as she realized what those three words implied.

"I don't know what to say," Callie replied, in a low tone. "It's all innocent."

Rebecca realized the sting of her words and the inherent truth in Callie that said she was not lying. She decided to look for a way to ease out of the awkwardness.

"You don't have to explain anything to me. He's just really fragile. I've been running interference all summer on the 'community' interest. I don't know what your risk is to be here. Just don't break his heart."

Callie and Rebecca were finding a common understanding. Although approaching and caring for the same man from different directions and for different reasons, their common goal of not creating a hurtful situation for him brought them closer together.

"Don't worry, I'm not here for anything like that," Callie confessed. "But to be honest, that WOULD even the score."

Callie took a quick pull on her cocktail while enjoying Rebecca's expression of surprise. Rebecca showed a smile as she began to see the true Callie that Jason was obviously holding out for. As Callie started to giggle at her comment, Rebecca tapped cups with hers to toast a sisterhood now established over a couple of cocktails on the beach.

"Ok now, interrogation over."

The unexpected words spoken by a familiar voice came in from behind Callie.

"Doctor," Jason declared, while pointing at Rebecca and putting his hand on Callie's shoulder. "Did you get your case history?"

"We're just talkin'," Callie replied.

Her comment was to both protect her new friend and to make Jason wonder what they were talking about. He studied both of them, noting that each was hiding a mischievous smile behind their plastic cup.

"Um hmm. I know what that means," he said, looking back and forth between the two. "She had my complete history before I even knew it."

"Well," Rebecca interrupted. "Obviously not all of it."

Rebecca gave Callie a quick look and a wink. Jason watched the nonverbal communication between the two new friends and wondered what was said.

"Are you hungry?" Jason asked as he turned to look at Callie.

The party was losing value as a good medium for softening the reunion between them. He knew that Callie's purpose for being there was not to share his social life. Further, he wanted time alone with her to talk and to finally have the conversation he had gone through in his head thousands of times over the years. It was one that he was afraid to have because he knew she would want an explanation for events past that he wasn't sure he wanted to share. But it was also a conversation he had ached for over the years when regretting his choice to run and wondering how her life without him had been, and who she was today.

Surprised by the sudden shift, Callie paused, then looked to Rebecca who nodded approval.

"I suppose I am," she answered in an aloof tone.

"Great!" he replied. "We can go get a bite at The Shack. Good food, cold beer, and t-shirt casual."

Callie's blank look showed no enthusiasm for Jason's suggestion. She again looked to Rebecca, who nodded that the restaurant's environment was suitable for them to get reacquainted with each other.

"OK then, let's go!" Callie answered, with a questioning enthusiasm that once again sought support from Rebecca through raised eyebrows.

Callie did not wait for a response as she started to walk toward the cottage while grabbing Jason's hand to get him moving. Her eagerness to move on from the party was not hidden by hesitation. She agreed that it was time for them to sit and to talk uninterrupted.

"Bye. Enjoyed talking with you," Callie said to Rebecca as she pulled Jason along like a reluctant child.

"Same. Y'all have fun," Rebecca answered, amused to watch her usually confident friend being so willingly directed away.

Up until this happy hour, Jason had been steadfast in not showing any interest in any woman, regardless of who presented interest in him. Rebecca thought his non-interest for some very legitimate prospects was due to his still stinging from his divorce. She thought he was gun-shy. Callie's presence changed her thinking. Jason was showing a vastly different demeanor. She watched as the two continued to walk down the beach, playfully bumping as Callie both accepted Jason's hand and arm around her then cast it off to start the process all over again.

"We didn't have to leave. I was having a good time," Callie said, feeling a twinge of guilt for taking Jason away from his friends with likely only a few parties left in the season.

"That's OK. It was my suggestion," Jason replied. "Besides, it was getting kind of weird."

"They're just curious. Rebecca wasn't prying. I mean, what's more intriguing than you showing up with me?"

Jason smiled but held his response to the comment. Callie pushed him off-stride to get him back into the conversation. He returned to her side but did not take her hand.

"They're just my favorite people here. I had to separate you from them," he answered apologetically. "I hope you don't mind."

"It's totally fine. Really. I didn't come here to make new friends."

Callie immediately regretted the comment, closing her eyes and dropping her face toward the sand. Jason stopped walking as her words finished. Running possible escape comments through her head, Callie took several seconds to think.

"Fuck," she mouthed softly towards the sand, feeling his eyes on her.

"And there it is," he mumbled, still looking at her look at the sand. "The elephant in the room."

Callie knew she should have been prepared for this situation, but she wasn't. Her plan was not to engage with him. It was just to see him. But the reality that one was going to happen as a result of the other wasn't as obvious to her then as it was now. There was no way Callie could uncover everything she sought just by seeing him from afar. And there was no way this question would not come up if and when they got the opportunity to talk.

"What?" seemed like the only appropriate volley back to him.

"The elephant in the room we've both been ignoring all day," Jason answered.

Callie's brain froze from the overload of trying to think through the middle area between what she wanted to say, what she could say, and what she should say to the man who crushed her heart and embarrassed her twenty-seven years ago just weeks before their wedding.

"Don't... please," was her unconscious answer to buy time.

"We have to talk about it at some point. Right?" Jason answered, pressing the moment. "So, why not now?"

Callie looked up to see Jason looking straight into her eyes. His demeanor had shifted to a seriousness she had not seen all day. The initial dancing and studying seemed to be ending as the search for honesty and truth was taking over.

"Seriously?" Callie responded.

"Easiest way is to clear the air."

His seven words seemed to soothe the tension within her. She looked at him to find faith that what she said would be in confidence and not used to either gain advantage or to hurt her again. The Jason she loved decades ago was not easy to read, particularly toward the end when the stresses overwhelmed him and eventually took them. His look was sincere, almost fearful. She decided to trust him again.

"I don't know why I'm here. Are you happy with that?!" she replied softly, not sure if she should be tough or vulnerable. "I got ditched by my husband for a buddies' golf weekend, saw on Facebook that you bought this place, and was drawn here. I suppose. I... I don't know."

Jason could see that her explanation had painful roots into her marriage. He knew from experience that unearthing that pain would remove Callie emotionally from the moments he wanted to have with her while she was there. He decided to give her an out to avoid the personal struggle with the truth he suspected she was having.

"Stop," he interjected softly. "Never mind. I'm not going to ruin this. I'm just glad you're here."

"Thank you," she replied, showing huge relief.

Jason sensed he was causing damage to the purpose of her visit by being so direct. He had to change tack to bring back the ease and friendliness that had existed between them until now.

"I really can't believe you're standing two feet from me," he said with a glow on his face. "I just don't know what to make of it."

Callie felt a twinge of anxiety return.

"How about nothing?" she answered. "Can't we just spend some time together? Catch up? Laugh. I'd really like to laugh."

Callie looked at him with the expression of warmth and friendship he hoped he would see if ever he had the opportunity to spend time with her again. Now, she was in front of him; and he could not blow the moment.

"Deal," came out quickly to preserve everything.

Callie's face showed immediate relief. Her body relaxed and the fear on her face evaporated. She had no way to verbalize her reason for being there. That was still working itself out in her head. But, in the same light, she knew the spontaneous decision to visit for the day was not wrong. It had to happen.

Jason started to put his arm around Callie to comfort her but pulled back in fear of overstepping. They finished their walk back to the stairs less playfully than how they started it. Their two eager dogs were waiting at the gate to greet them.

## 7

The Shack was a landmark building built on the sound's water edge that had a view that soaked in sunsets. During the summer, the wait for tables was hours. The crowd started before noon and rolled through until well after midnight. Live music, and a livelier dance, floor was its signature, having hosted local band favorites and imports from around the southeast and mid-Atlantic. Parking was usually a challenge when arriving, often dependent on the fortunate timing to someone leaving. Pulling into the parking lot often amused Jason, reminding him of a life-lesson saying he embedded in his kids when they were young, and he was trying to find a parking spot. *Winners find parking spaces.*

The Jeep kicked up a cloud of dust as it left the pavement and hit the sandy surface of the lot. A lucky space appeared near the front door and Jason immediately swung into it as if it had been waiting for him. Callie was enjoying the ride in the open Jeep, reliving younger days with Jason when they drove around in his Jeep CJ7. As they came to a stop, the plume of dust that followed them settled off into the distant lot. Callie took a moment to compose herself.

"This thing reminds me of when we were driving back to my house through Georgetown in the pouring rain with that little, worthless top you had on it."

"The bikini top," Jason replied.

"Aptly named." Callie smirked, recalling that it did not cover much of anything.

"We got soaked. I think there was an inch of water in the car," Jason recalled, visualizing the pond of water on his floorboards. "Your housemates did us a good by having the driveway and a garage spot cleared when we got to the house."

"They did, didn't they?"

Callie never told Jason that she was surprised they made the effort.

"I miss those guys. I haven't seen them since. Haven't thought of them either... Crazy. They likely live near me now."

Thinking of her old housemates and the time that had passed since gave her a somber feeling. She moved back to Cleveland from DC when she and Jason became engaged. That was the separation point with her old friends that did not come back together when she returned a year later. At that time, she was introduced to Chase, who was already established, redirecting her time and attention to his world rather than to rebuild her old one that attached to Jason. She made a mental note to search Facebook for her old housemates.

"Yup," Callie said out loud, while twirling around to view her ride. "This takes me back."

# # #

The building that housed *The Shack* had a weathered wood-plank shell and metal roof. Its crooked front door completed the presentation that lived up to its name and beach party reputation. Live, loud country music radiated through its exterior and filled the parking lot to set the mood.

As the door opened, the bustle inside became visible and the music grew dramatically louder. Jason smiled as he looked to Callie to get her first impression of what *The Shack* was proving to be. As they worked their way into the crowd that flowed around them, Jason pointed to the rear of the building that hosted a large wooden deck filled with tables and people.

The hostess walked them through the maze of activity and presented a table for two by the rail. She handed them some menus, then disappeared back into the crowd.

"This was lucky," Callie observed, as she looked around while sitting down. "The perfect table on the perfect night."

"WINNERS... get great tables," Jason replied sarcastically, while pushing in her chair.

"And find parking spaces."

"That too," he confirmed, with a smile thinking about all the times he and his kids would 'say the phrase' when going to places with tight parking.

"I'll bet you dinner this is your regular table," Callie challenged, noticing that the path in was too easy and that the perfect table just happened to be available.

Jason toasted his water glass to the notion. Callie lifted her glass to touch his.

"Think you got me all figured out?" he asked, with a smirk, knowing full well she was comparing the old Jason she remembered with the present one in front of her. That thought came to him because he was doing it too.

"I thought I had you figured out twenty-seven years ago, and you left me," she answered before realizing she was throwing a damp rag on the night. "I'm not so sure about you today. I'm workin' on this version."

Jason found her remark honest and amusing. A sign they were getting somewhere. There was a lot he wanted to tell her. But he was not sure if she was either interested in or up to knowing what he was thinking.

"That shouldn't be hard. I'm an open book," he declared to invite her questions.

Callie listened to the implied invitation and thought about the opportunity to really drill in. But she knew that would come with consequences. There was a quid pro quo to his proposition. He would want to know as much from her, which she was not yet sure she wanted to share. Jason had a confident and happy look on his face. She had to knock him down a bit.

"Open book? I think we both know that's a load of crap," she contested. "Prove it."

Jason nodded in appreciation as Callie toasted her water glass back at him. He clinked her glass to accept the challenge as their waitress arrived.

"Hey, Jason," the waitress said in a familiar and friendly tone. "Your regular?"

Jason noticed Callie relishing the attention he was getting. Stuck, he started to laugh at the awkwardness.

"Yes... that'd be great," he replied near laughter, conceding his loss of the bet. "Rainey, this is Callie. Callie, Rainey."

Callie smiled through the introduction to say hello to Jason's friend.

"Nice to meet you, Callie. How about you?"

Callie tried to remain composed but found her glee in being right overtaking her expression. She took a sip from her water to hide her elation.

"Dinner's on you," she said, looking over the glass ridge towards Jason. "You're such a liar."

# # #

The dinner crowd had thinned to smaller groups of young and old, drinking, laughing, and rotating inside and out to dance and to find the restrooms. Jason, remembering Callie's reluctance at the beach, was avoiding anything related to the big question of why she was there. Callie was equally cautious to figure out the best way to learn what she wanted to know about him without leaving herself vulnerable to the questions she either could not or didn't want to answer.

"Thank you. That was really good," Callie said, breaking an awkward silence between them. She was as relaxed as she would ever be and was now ready to talk.

"You know we've been talking an awful lot about nothing," she added to orient the discussion to what she wanted to know.

"That was our deal. I can keep going all night if you'd like. I'm really good at it."

Jason lifted his beer for a clink. He was amused by the sexual innuendo in his comment, waiting to see if Callie would put it together. She took it for what he meant and just looked at him to get serious.

"This is so crazy. I feel like I've known you forever. But I have no idea who you are now," she started. "It's like no time has passed. I'm so comfortable here. Is that weird?"

Jason took a moment to think about her comment. It was true that over the past thirty-plus years, they dated and were engaged for three and apart for almost twenty-eight. That was the first time he had ever put their history into a time-lined perspective. She was always Callie to him. Present tense. Their relationship, despite the fact that he had a twenty-four-year-old daughter along with three others, seemed like yesterday.

"I don't know if it's weird. But I get it," he replied. "You knew me a long time ago for a short period of time. I've changed. As I'm sure you have too. But I'll be an open book to you. You can ask me anything."

"Anything?" Callie asked, almost giddy with the potential.

"Yes, anything."

"Realllly?" she asked as she relished the thought and began thinking about where to start. "OK, Mr. Open Book... This'll be fun. Let's start with easy ones... Where are your girls?"

Jason gave her a strange look. The question was not what he expected and surprised him to be oriented to his family with another woman.

"Right now?" he asked playfully. "I don't quite know. It's Saturday night."

Callie rolled her eyes in disappointment. Mr. Open Book did what she expected by evading the question.

"Funny. You know what I mean."

Jason did not get the play-along he was hoping for as Callie dug in to pursue her line of questioning. He knew his best option was to simply answer her questions.

"Fair enough," he conceded, while sitting up for the cross-examination. "Ready? This may take a while."

Callie leaned forward to listen.

"Rachel, number one, lives in Houston, Texas working as a paralegal at a big multinational law firm dealing with intellectual property theft by the Chinese. She plans on going to law school, likely somewhere in Texas. Elise, number two, just graduated from Drexel in Philly and is working for the government trying to reshape the city into something green. I really don't know what that means, but I'm all for it. Faith, number three, is at Virginia in neuro studies. Our brain studying the brain, so to speak. She'll be a doctor. Rebecca, who you met at the beach, loves that and can't wait to meet her. And Maya, my youngest, is a sophomore studying business, I hope, maybe education. Which way is the wind blowing today?"

Callie smiled at the automated roll-through of his girls.

"You've been busy. And I love the names. Where's Maya in school?"

"NC State," he answered.

"That's convenient to here."

Jason started easing. "That it is... and will be in-state tuition at some point. She pops in now and then. Usually unannounced."

Callie felt an uneasiness hit her stomach.

"Will I be a problem if she shows tonight?"

"I'm not going to lie so... probably," Jason answered. "But it's late. That window has passed. Should I be concerned about an angry husband's Porsche flying into my driveway?"

Callie laughed in nervous response. The question was so cavalier, inappropriate, and so Jason.

"Maserati," she replied, happy to make the correction. "And, I don't think you have to worry. He likely won't even think about where I am."

Jason rolled his eyes at the Maserati reference then gave a comforting look to the veiled confession and hurt Callie was obviously feeling. She showed an immediate regret for hinting at Chase's lack of attention, then decided to keep her focus on Jason to avoid any follow-up questions.

"Enough of that," she blurted. "What about your EX?"

"What about her?" Jason answered, surprised by the question. "She won't be showing up either."

Callie laughed at the response she did not expect.

"Figured that," she replied, adding, "although that would certainly make things interesting. I'd certainly have some questions for her. What's she like?"

Callie noticed Jason was uncomfortable with the question. He and Stephanie ended amicably after many years of a bad and declining relationship. He was uncertain if he should be honest or sugarcoat it, hoping to make it boring enough for Callie to want to move on.

"Really?" he asked to confirm her interest to know.

Callie did not either respond or budge from a stare that stated she wanted an answer.

"You know the story of the princess and the pea, right?" Jason asked, raising his eyebrows.

Callie visualized the fairytale illustration of *The Princess and the Pea* who complained about the discomfort caused by a pea under her mattress despite having many mattresses stacked on it to eliminate any possible feel or discomfort. The visualization gave Callie a tinge of sympathy for him.

"Oh," was all she could think to say.

"That's unfair," Jason added. "She was a terrific wife and mother. She just wanted different things and everything her way."

Callie was intrigued to learn more but decided that it had to be Jason's choice to offer. It was not her right to seek more detail through questions. She let his last comment hang.

"See her much?"

"Not at all," he answered. "We don't even speak unless it's a kid issue that usually involves money. But she's in Cleveland. Happy. I guess. Dating. I'm sure. Last few years we stayed together while Maya was still home. It was rough for everyone but necessary for Maya. But we're good now. One thing for sure, full disclosure, was our life was really up and down. We were broke or just making it far more often than having anything. I got lucky with the last business. Bottom-of-the-ninth home run. Right idea, right place, right time, and certainly the right environment."

There was a lot to digest in his answer. From Callie's Facebook snoops, the only presentation of Jason and his family were happy as family, during the usual holidays and life celebrations, or athletics with his girls. There were no signs that he lived an unhappy life or that his career struggled. The misleading images always created some jealousy in her.

"I'm sure luck had nothing to do with any of it," she responded, trying to ease the moment. "Good or bad."

Jason was lost in thought, visualizing occurrences over his life. His head was shaking side to side as he ran a mental review of his married life.

"It wasn't easy... and, to her credit, she held in there," he answered.

"I'm sorry. I'm being too nosey," Callie declared to stop his discomfort. "I'm just curious to see where you are."

"I'm right here," he answered. "Right in front of you. What you see is what you get."

Callie was happy to see his face shift back from discomfort to engagement. She wanted to bring up a time when Stephanie had crossed paths with her family. It was humorous. So, the timing seemed right.

"You know my mom met her," Callie offered, watching closely for his response.

Her new direction relieved Jason. He smiled as the memory reappeared in his head.

"I DO KNOW THAT. At Jane's baby shower. I thought it was hilarious," he answered. "But she was mortified. I think she was, like, eight months pregnant with Rachel."

Callie was happy to see Jason's amused reply. Although, when it happened, it hurt. Jason had finally moved on from her and was about to have a child with someone else. That realization, even though she married someone else before he married, was a dark cloud that followed her long after she heard about it.

"I got the full report," Callie said, reliving the pain but able to hold a happy face.

Jason was oblivious to Callie's hidden emotion and wanted more information.

"And?" he asked, pushing for details.

"My mom actually liked her," she confessed, which was true. "She said she was polite and nice and likely had no idea who Mother was... or what a dick she had married... KIDDING!"

Callie's joke stunned Jason as she rolled into a heavy laughter. She watched his face go blank as her eyes teared, reigniting her laughter again. After a few stops and restarts, she worked to regain her composure, then wiped her eyes dry. Jason eventually found Callie's comment mildly funny, acknowledging it with a smirk instead of a smile.

"Nice," he replied. "Steph had no idea she was next to your mom. You should have seen her face when I told her that nice woman, named Carolyn, a friend of my mother's, was your mom..."

The humor in it all evaporated with the mental vision created by his comment. Baby showers are supposed to be a fun time for everyone. And, despite the funny awkward situation created by the overlap of worlds at a mutual friend's celebration, it was still sad for Jason to think about. His face went blank as he thought more deeply into what it all meant.

"I'm sorry. I didn't..." Callie said, trying to pull him back from the funk she created.

Jason waved off the issue as he collected himself. This was not a time to reflect on past sadness. He had the time he wanted with Callie that could end at any minute. He did not want it filled with either sadness or awkward reflections.

"I'm done," Callie said to put an end to her questioning.

She knew from Jason's responses that he still held emotional ties back to his ex-wife and the life experiences they shared. She also knew he was excited to see her and to be with her that day. And she felt the same about him. But the time had come to let him off the hook and to stop asking about his backstory. Their time together was now, and the clock was ticking. She had no predetermined plan for her exit. But she knew that the time to go would come, and she wanted their time together to be healthy and fun.

Jason showed relief in Callie's declaration that her probing questions had ended. Nervously, he repositioned some of the table items in front of him. He then looked to her with a renewed vigor and interest to share.

"Well... that was easy," he declared sarcastically as he moved his water glass onto a paper coaster. "Now, it's your turn."

After letting him off the hook, Callie did not expect the questioning to come back at her. A panic tightened her stomach and radiated up through her shoulders. She felt her lips pinched together as his eyes focused in on hers.

"What?" was all that she could say while beginning to feel a new pressure.

"YOU. Your story," Jason answered, in a glib tone. "Fill me in on your last twenty-seven years. I know you're dying to tell me."

The initial tension subsided as Callie thought about what she would share. Unable to frame a good story, she volleyed the question back to him.

"What do you want to know?"

Callie was doing her best to hold her composure. But Jason could see that the confidence she was trying to convey was being undermined by nervousness. It fascinated him to learn about her life adventures. Her life and marriage to Chase touched highest level, Republican party, national politics. But he made a silent commitment to himself to stop anything that either got too emotional or had the potential to end their time together.

"Where are your kids?" he asked, thinking it was safe to start with. "Three, right?"

The fear that had overcome her seemed to evaporate with the question. Callie smiled and waved her hand as she replied.

"Well, it's Saturday night..." she answered smugly to mock him.

"Seriously?" he asked with a smile. "That's my joke."

"One of few worth stealing," she answered with a pause to watch his face. "Sorry... YES... three... Michael just graduated from UVA. Will is a junior at William and Mary. Lizzie is a freshman at James Madison. But you likely know that."

Callie amused herself thinking about her similar machine-gun synopsis of children as Jason waved off her accusation of him knowing about her children already. Of course, he knew that. Although Callie was not an avid Facebook poster, she completed enough of her profile section to list and link to her husband and three children.

"Did you ever think we'd have college-age kids?" he asked to encourage her to continue. "Those are all really good schools, and in-state too. Very nice. Studying?"

Callie showed no hesitation to answer the question. She was eager to fill in the gaps on her accomplished children. She went through the list from oldest to youngest. Her son Michael was a Spanish major, now teaching English in Madrid. He was away until Christmas. Her second son, Will, was a political science major looking at law school. Lizzie, her baby and only daughter, was undecided with no major declared. But children and education appeared to be her direction. In summary, they were all happy where they were. So, she was happy.

Callie stopped to take a drink as she watched Jason digest her answer and tee-up his next question. She was happy that her overview of her children was consistent to the level of his. Both held concern that their children's success would not measure up to the other's. Jason remained silent as Callie ended her family's history noting there was one person she left out.

"And?" was all he had to ask to freeze her mid-gulp.

Callie slowly returned her cup to the table while looking at him with squinted eyes. She was trying to determine if he truly wanted to know anything or if he was just trying to get a rise out of her.

"Really?" she asked, not quite willing to surrender information too easily. After all, he had left her long before she gave him the ring back.

"I told you mine," he smirked.

"I'm married to the guy I met after I dumped you."

Callie knew that would sting. His knowledge of her and her family showed, at a minimum, that he had creeped on her Facebook for information relative to her family and husband. He knew the answers to the questions he was asking.

"Ouch again," he answered, confirming the direct hit.

Callie was amused by his reaction and did not hesitate to show it. But she was also sensitive to his feelings and wanted to dial back the accusation to what truly happened.

"Ok, after you and I 'separated,'" she corrected and waited for him to begin breathing again. "Five weeks before our wedding date."

There was no letting go of the fact that the separation caused an enormous amount of embarrassment to Callie and her family. Their marriage was not the typical union of two ordinary people. It was a social event in one of Cleveland's most prominent communities, uniting two established families with overlapping friends and social groups. The union was one of high celebratory anticipation for the season. The destruction of it, particularly so close to the ceremony, sent shock waves through the community. Because she was living at home, Callie was caught in the middle. Jason, however, was insulated, living in their soon-to-be-home in a gentrified riverfront community near the city.

"Yes, I remember those details," he answered, looking to move past that hurtful time. "What does he do?"

"Chase? He fixes and manages political campaigns, congressional and senate, mostly in the southeast. He's the RNC's go-to GUY," Callie answered, knowing full well that Jason knew that too.

"I knew who he was and where he worked when you started dating him," Jason confirmed. "Everyone was dying to tell me. Surprised he still does it."

Jason's mockery of Chase's single-path career was not lost on Callie. Jason's career had been all over the place, which seemed exciting but at a very high risk for success.

"He loves it," she responded, ignoring the insinuation. "Funny how everyone thinks it's important to share details of exes even years after a split. You know how I found out about you being here?"

"Sandy," Jason answered in a matter-of-fact tone.

Jason knew all of his social media overlaps with Callie from the occasional comments she would make that he could see.

"That's right! How'd you know that?" she answered.

Jason smiled as he moved his glass without taking a drink. The action was to give Callie time to process that Sandy was the common acquaintance that created the opportunity for them to meet a second time over thirty years ago. The deeper conversation on exactly when they first met was an ongoing debate during their courtship and engagement.

Jason remembered meeting Callie years before they started dating while standing in a buffet line at Lake Shores Golf Club in Cleveland. In between them was Callie's father. Callie's oldest sister Patty and Jason attended separate, but affiliated, small Virginia liberal arts colleges at the same time. His parents were casual friends with her mom and dad. Jason had just graduated from college and was in his first year of consulting. Callie, being five years younger, had just completed high school. Any interest from him for her at that point would not have gone well.

Jason recalled Callie standing behind her father in the buffet line when he was introduced to her. Her response was one of complete disinterest, which amused him now and was likely the reason she never recalled it happening. She was noticeably pouting at having to be there, which he found attractive in itself.

That one, brief moment, however, had stayed with him during his out-of-town work and travels over the next several years. He was excited to cross paths with her again through Sandy when Callie was older, in art school, and more interested in getting to know him. By that time, Jason had left the consulting world to find new opportunity.

"Sandy's one of our few common social media overlaps. I just figured you saw my post."

"She actually showed it to me. I don't know why," Callie replied.

Her comment amused him.

"You can always count on Sandy."

And he did.

"Anyway. Chase's... Chase? Sounds like a cool gig."

Jason wanted to keep the conversation away from his Facebook account, not wanting Callie to think about his latest post and her as the ultimate target for it. He was more interested in talking through her life to see if what he thought was her life now actually was her life now. Callie did not immediately respond.

"It's cool for him," she said directly, then tailed off with, "Pays obscenely well. But..."

"He's away a lot?" Jason completed her thought, which didn't annoy her this time. He got it and was not using her answer to make an inquiry on her availability.

"Yup," she answered abruptly, looking off into the darkness and hoping not to be seen as vulnerable.

"That sucks," Jason observed, looking to spin positive. "Meet the president?"

"Presidents," she answered, perking up to qualify her response. "Plural. W and the Donald. Oh, and HW after he was out of office."

Jason smiled as he saw light return to her face.

"That's fun. Away this weekend?"

The light that lit started to fade. He regretted the question the moment he asked it.

"Mmm hm. But golfing."

"Work?"

"With his buddies," she answered, while shaking her head in disappointment.

"That's right. You said that earlier," he replied, regretting having opened the wound again. "I was never a golfer. What's he like? Better, who would he remind me of?"

"Why?"

Callie thought his question was strange and difficult to answer without either puffing Chase up or making him seem less than he was.

"Just asking."

Jason liked to use aligning people to celebrities as a tactic when discussing people, particularly referrals, in business. The answer was almost always skewed more to personality than physical appearance. He was interested to know if Chase was like him, or someone completely different. Callie knew it was bugging him.

"I think I'll just leave you hanging on that one," she replied, almost gleeful in withholding. "I don't want to scare you."

"I can take it," he answered sarcastically. "I'm just interested to know who, or what for that matter, won your heart."

"Yeah, well, tough shit," she answered, now gleaming ear to ear with the secret she knew was bugging him more than any. "I'm just going to let you wonder."

Callie reclined back in her chair, signaling to Jason she would not open everything to discussion. He remembered her stubborn side that would hold tight on anything she set her mind to keep to herself. When they were together, he did have some success chiseling away and finally getting what he wanted to know. But that always took time and, more so, a lot of trust. Neither of which he had right now. He decided to laugh it off for a later try.

"You can tell me later," he said to close that conversation with an expectation to talk about it again. "Let's change the subject. How's your mom? Better? How are your lovely sisters? Do they ask about me? I don't think they ever liked me."

Callie started laughing as the pressure and anxiety she was feeling started to ease. His questions were ridiculous. It would mortify her mother to hear that the two were even talking. His sisters never really liked him as a spouse for her. But his antics were becoming borderline desperate as he maneuvered for information. That lightened the mood and created a much-improved setting for the night ahead.

"Enough!" she cried out, trying to stop from smiling while, at the same time, trying to egg him on. Things were starting to come together to show who he really was now, which was a calmer version of the man she loved back then.

## 8

The homes along the shoreline were lit with a white sheen from the low-hanging moon as the Jeep rolled past in the shadows. Jason was quiet. He was sad, expecting that their arrival back at the cottage would end Callie's visit. The drive back to Williamsburg was two hours of highway that would get her home before her mother went to bed. He visualized that greeting in his head along with the loving interrogation Callie would have to endure to explain her sudden trip to the shore. Callie would have to compose a story that did not include him.

As the Jeep pulled into the driveway, the music got louder as it echoed in the space under the cottage. Jason turned off the motor, which silenced the song halfway through its chorus. They both remained still in their seats. Neither unlatched their seat belt.

"This has been really fun," Jason said quietly, as he looked straight ahead.

He did not want to look at Callie, fearing it would start the process of saying goodbye and become the last time he would ever see her.

"It has been. Thank you," she replied, waiting for his eyes to roll from the darkness to look at her.

Jason knew if he turned his head that tears would flow to create an embarrassing moment. The time with her was just as he imagined it would be. Magical. It was the same feeling he felt in the buffet line and when they met again a few years later. But now the situation was different. She was with him, but not free to be with him. It was clear she had no plans when she arrived at his home and was likely expected back in Williamsburg.

"If you're driving back to Williamsburg, you should get going. You'll get there around eleven."

It had to be said. It was painful to suggest, knowing the answer and result it would create. He turned to find her looking down into the darkness of the Jeep's floorboard.

"I should. Yes, I should," Callie answered matter-of-factly. "But, ya know? I honestly don't want to."

As she spoke, she looked up and laughed nervously, knowing its insinuation. But all she wanted was for the conversation to continue. They had found an emotional peace between them she wanted to explore. Staying the night might imply a night together. But, deep inside, Callie knew Jason would respect her. That, regardless of what he was feeling, he would attempt nothing improper. She felt safe with the suggestion that she would stay.

"You're welcome to stay in my guestroom. We can go get whatev—"

"I have what I need," Callie responded, relieved that she was right about him.

"Even better! The guest room was the first thing completed to get my girls to visit. So, it's only fitting that my former fiancée beats three of the four to that room."

Jason kept talking to fill the silence so she could not change her mind. When he finished his comment, he hoped to see a smile gleaming back at him. But all he got was a nervous expression. Realization had set in that she just committed to a secret overnight stay with her former lover. The man she had once been committed to marry. A situation that, if uncovered, would destroy the trust and bond of her marriage. Callie began to doubt her decision.

"I accept your offer," she finally said, after a brief pause to decide to push through her concern and guilt.

"Done," Jason proclaimed with a like fear of her changing her mind. "The complete Cartwright Columbus Day package. Say that three times fast. And... ya know what? It's still early. Maybe some live music? And maybe even... some dancing?"

"Sounds great," Callie answered in a diminished voice, faintly smiling and looking forward to a fun night with him. "But let me go get dressed a bit better."

Jason smiled at her comment. Callie was going to dress up for him. However, the place he had in mind did not require a change of attire. It was frequented mostly by locals and therefore, local casual.

"You don't have to," he said, taking a moment to admire her. "It's T, well, sweatshirts now, and shorts here. You look great as you are."

Callie laughed off the compliment.

"No, Jason, you look great in your sweatshirt and shorts, and that killer tan." She stopped to take in the golden image in front of her. "The rest of us have to work on it a bit."

Jason followed her up the stairs to the cottage to unlock the door. As he reached around her for the doorknob, she turned to face him. For the first time in twenty-seven years, their faces were within inches of each other. Callie nibbled on her bottom lip as she looked into his eyes, then down to his mouth. She leaned closer to smell the familiar musk of his skin as she kissed him softly on the lips. Her lips pinched on his lower lip as it did decades ago, then pulled outward lightly as she pulled away. She watched him as they separated, and as his eyes reopened.

"What was that about?" he asked, still buzzed by her impulsive touch. "I was just reaching for the door."

In hindsight, Jason would decide that the kiss should have been expected once the overnight was accepted. If Callie was with him and at the point to leave, her contact would have been a hug to keep the visit sterile. But she kissed him. And it was just as out of the blue as their first kiss on their first date together. When that happened, she said she just wanted to get it out of the way to let him know it was fine if he wanted to kiss her back. He did. Callie found Jason's embarrassed surprise amusing and comforting.

"Don't get any big ideas. I was just wondering if this version tastes better than what I remember."

"And?"

Callie smiled and did not answer. Jason knew from history that either he would never know or only be given bits and pieces to put together for the answer. He opened the door for her to go change. The dogs were waiting to join him outside.

"I'll be out on the deck," he said, as she walked off.

As he started toward the water, he thought about whether he should be happy about what just happened. And, as Callie disappeared into the darkness of the hallway back to the bedrooms, she stopped to look back to see Jason lost in thought midway down the walkway. The kiss was impulsive and sent a lot of mixed signals. She regretted it for a moment thinking about all the possible ramifications if uncovered. She then licked her lips again, having savored the feel and taste of his.

The sliding door had a distinct noise when it opened quickly. Jason was standing at the end of the walkway with the two dogs at his side when Callie made her reappearance. Zoe immediately turned, followed by Molly. Both ran to greet then escort her back down the walkway. Jason turned slowly with the moonlight behind him, anxious to compare the real with what he imagined he would see.

Callie remembered that Jason loved her look best when she was natural. His informality was his greatest appeal. She appeared in knee-length linen shorts complemented by a flowy, quarter-zip bamboo-cotton sweatshirt. Her hair was straight and hung just as it used to be when they were together. His eyes lit to the sight of her as he exhaled into a smile as she walked closer.

"Wow. I must be dreaming," he said, stepping forward to better admire her look.

Callie playfully finished her approach with a few bouncy steps and a twirl to show all her angles.

"I have to be ready to go out when I visit my mom."

"To be seen?"

"To be seen. To impress," she answered.

Callie twirled again and laughed in appreciation for Jason's adoration of her in that moment. It was exhilarating to feel that she could still attract the complete focus of a man. Her relationship with Chase had become too routine. He rarely complimented her look or choices of attire despite the effort she would put in to creating something he would like.

"Well, mission accomplished. On both," he declared.

Jason's appreciation was genuine. It would take a moment for him to realize, but Callie's presence stopped his breathing. He smiled at the thought when he took his next breath. He knew the look she created was for him and would not be the outfit she would choose for a dinner out in Williamsburg with her mother. As he walked toward her, a twinge of concern hit his conscience that what was happening may not be a good thing for either of them. He had to be more careful in his behavior and expectations. He had to position it so that regardless of the end result, he and Callie would be on the best possible terms for the future instead of back with a wall between them.

The country music coming from behind the wooden doors blended with the party buzz permeating from the outside deck that sat behind the building. Jason pulled into a close, hidden parking space that he often found open even during the high season. He immediately hopped out to run around the Jeep to help Callie out of the vehicle.

The crowd inside was dense and enjoying the band that, to Callie's ear, played fun country music. On the dance floor, a line dance was in motion with upwards of twenty men and women moving in unison to the music. Jason grabbed Callie's hand to navigate them to the bar to order. Knowing there was no chance to tell him what she wanted to drink, Callie raised two fingers for him to order for her what he was having. She then looked around and pointed to the outside deck.

The warm temperature that appeared after the rain was cooling as the breeze continued to hold the bugs at bay. The night's setting was perfect, and the music was muffled enough to make talking possible. As Jason and Callie sat at a rail-side table overlooking the water, both felt the night could not more perfectly reflect the happiness both were finding in spending time together.

"Band's great!" Callie commented, trying to open the conversation.

"Locals. You should know a lot of their stuff," Jason responded awkwardly, not knowing where to go in conversation.

The silence continued as each looked around, trying to find a topic of conversation that could help advance the evening. As they would catch the other's eyes, smiles would emerge simultaneously on both their faces, hiding their angst to find more interesting things to talk about. After a few minutes that seemed like thirty, Jason slapped his hand on the table.

"Ok," he said, looking around as if that action would mysteriously create a topic of interest for them.

Callie waited for his follow-up when the band stopped.

"All right, gentlemen, we're going to slow it down A LOT," was announced over the sound system and received by a number of hoots and whistles. "So, here's your chance. Don't be shy to ask that girl you've been eyein' for a dance."

Callie immediately clamped her lips from smiling as she shook her head in disbelief. The timing of the slow dance seemed divinely scheduled. Although she was drawn to Jason, kissed him, and had agreed to stay overnight in his house, the thought of a slow dance, the casual foreplay that could lead to all sorts of things not good for her, made her more nervous than the other three things combined. Slow dancing was close touching, romantic and rhythmic. It was a place where pretending could stop. Callie looked to Jason for understanding, only to instead find him standing with his hand extended for hers.

"I love this song," he said calmly. "And you promised me a dance."

Callie's body tightened. She wanted to dance again with someone who was not mechanical and distant as Chase was now, like she did with Jason long ago, and with Chase for a while after their marriage.

"I agreed to listen to music," she responded, hoping that would be enough to dissuade his interest. But instead, he stepped closer.

"Please," he asked again, placing his hand within inches of hers.

Callie hesitated, then took his hand and stood. The song was slow and melodic. The lyrics pierced through the feelings that each was having. Jason initially held Callie loosely. He was respectful to show to her that it was just a slow dance and not going any further. Callie felt a rush of relaxation flow through her body as her movement coordinated with his within a space where two people cannot avoid contact. The touch of his hand to hers, his leg brushing on hers, and his body so close to hers was intoxicating. As the dance continued, the music and crowd around them evaporated as they held each other tighter, narrowing the distance between them until it was gone.

When the song ended, Callie and Jason returned to the reality of their surroundings. Both were slow to separate from the other, and embarrassed to look at the other. Jason touched his forehead to hers.

"Thank you."

"For what?" she responded, feeling hot with perspiration and blushing.

"For coming."

After digging into his pocket, Jason turned and pointed to the lead singer who gave him a return nod. He then walked to him, looking for a high five. At first, Callie thought it was an embarrassing, old-man gesture until she saw the money change hands as the next song started with an upbeat pace. Jason continued to bop with the music as he turned to leave the floor with Callie. When he did not find her where he had left her, he looked deeper on to the dancefloor to see her twirling around. A 'no' headshake and finger gesture calling him back onto the floor was an invitation he was not going to decline. Country music was perfect for soft contact dancing. Staying on the dancefloor also kept them in the right place for the next slow song.

## 9

The villa for their thirtieth anniversary outing was just like all the others they had rented over the years. With four bedrooms and three baths, it was perfect for eight guys who just needed a place to pass out after grinding out thirty-six holes of golf and finishing with big steak dinners and free-flowing booze. Despite all of them being in their mid-fifties, they could still party hard with only the added expectation that their recovery each morning would be more painful and take longer than it did ten, let alone thirty years ago.

Chase was working his way through the kitchen, grazing on various items Callie would have thrown out. With a full stomach from dinner and several double bourbons already in him, he realized that he had not either called or heard from his wife since their call the night before. With everyone in the living room focused on the Georgia–Clemson football game, he slipped out unnoticed to the back patio to check in and to see how her day had gone with *her mom*.

Chase instructed Siri to call Callie. He was anxious to see if and how she would answer the phone. Carolyn should have long since gone to bed, leaving Callie and Molly watching television. That Callie had not called him today was no surprise. She had a history of letting him hang himself on lesser matters. This call had to come from him. Getting her voicemail was not a good sign.

"Hey, it's me," he said carefully, trying to think through what to say and to not slur his words. "I'm just checking in to make sure you're not still mad. We'll talk when I get home. Love you."

Chase hung up, puzzled that Callie did not answer. His phone showed 10:15 p.m. She and Carolyn had to be home, and, if home, Carolyn was likely in bed. Maybe this time he had gone too far. He sat alone in the darkness of the patio when the sliding door opened.

"There you are, man," John Sabastian cried out with his mouth full of food and a bourbon in his hand. "Second half is starting."

John, known as Sabby since middle school, hailed from Selma, Alabama and had been Chase's roommate for three years in the Kappa Gamma house at Clemson. John's family was deeply embedded in Republican politics and extraordinarily helpful to Chase when he got started in DC. The family's connections also accelerated the development of Chase's reputation and business running campaigns throughout the southeast.

Sabby, like his daddy and granddaddy, was a lawyer. Callie found him repulsive with his short physique that carried 300 pounds. More so, she disliked his mantra that the more you eat and drink, the better off you are. Chase always gained weight when the two were together.

Chase's thoughts of Callie evaporated as he looked toward his college friend and his glass of bourbon. He turned off his phone and returned to the party for the second half of the game.

# # #

The music they were enjoying filled the air before Jason pulled his Jeep onto the parking pad under his cottage. It again went silent as he turned off the engine. Both he and Callie smiled at each other as they unclicked their seat belts and hopped out to walk towards the stairs. Still singing the lyrics to the song, Jason took Callie's hand to twirl her around a few times until she stumbled into his arms. The intoxication of the moment was not from the alcohol. It was the freshness of being together and carefree, if only for the moment.

Callie went to settle on the bench overlooking the water as Jason went into the cottage to release the dogs and to open a bottle of wine. The dogs scampered by with a quick look and sniff then headed down on to the beach, which Callie now accepted as normal. As she leaned forward to watch them frolic on the sand, Jason placed a blanket around her shoulders.

"This will keep you warm," he said, sitting down next to her. "And, this will also keep you warm."

He handed her a glass of Merlot from a bottle he had received as a gift that he had been saving for a special occasion. Callie took a taste, then leaned into him as the rich flavor permeated her taste buds. She watched his face show satisfaction from her touch while his eyes focused on the water and the dogs.

"Will Molly be OK?" she asked, simply to start the conversation.

"She'll be fine," he answered. "Zoe will keep tabs on her."

"Maybe we should buy glow-sticks for their collars. That's how we kept tabs on the kids in Nan-tuck—et."

Callie realized too late in her comment that she was now confusing families.

"That's a good idea," Jason answered with a slight smile. "I'll make a mental note to get some."

Callie knew the mix-up did not get past him and appreciated his not taking the opportunity to make a Nantucket funny. She relaxed in his confidence that Zoe would tend to Molly to keep her safe. It was not lost on her that Jason was also taking care of her today, respectful of everything that was in play.

Many aspects of the day could have turned sour. Callie being there was a sign that could have opened many improper thoughts to what could evolve between them. But she was not worried. It was Jason. The man she was going to marry and trust everything to. And, although that ended in disaster, there was something new and more in the current version of the man that confirmed she could trust him implicitly for respect, security, and secrecy through the days and nights of her stay, and into the future.

"This is perfect," she said quietly, as if to herself.

"Why do you say that?"

"It's just what I need right now."

"A short-term 'fix'?"

Jason regretted the sarcasm as fast as he said it.

"Can we just leave it at perfect?"

Her response was soft and unfazed by his glib reply.

"Perfect is good."

Relieved, Jason began to play with her hair as her head rested on his chest. Enjoying the playful touch that she had not felt in years from Chase, Callie smiled.

"Is this bad?" she asked.

Her question was as much rhetorical as it was to seek an answer from Jason. Jason knew this was a tipping point where an honest answer would likely bring her back to the reality of her being there, whereas a different answer might throw a wedge of distrust between them. Callie was looking for confirmation. Not insight. He had to be thoughtful.

"I can only speak for myself," he answered.

Surprised by the words he chose, Callie repositioned to look at him.

"If I were your wife and was doing this," she stated in a slow cadence. "Would this be bad?"

Jason could not avoid the answer he had to give. His chest deflated, knowing the impact his honesty would have.

"Without a doubt."

"What!? Why would you say that?" she answered in surprise.

"Because it's true. Do you want me to lie to you?"

Jason was equally surprised that Callie was seeking confirmation of something else.

"But that's me, as a husband. From this angle now, you with me here? No... for you, that is. You're safe," he finished.

Callie's face eased with his words. Without saying it, he just defined his expectations from her and for their time together. She was safe. That was all she needed to hear to feel comfortable that her time with him would not violate anything.

"That's better," she answered, easing Jason's anxiety. "Why'd you get divorced?"

Jason's blood pressure that had dropped with Callie's acceptance of his answer spiked again with her follow-up question. The reason for his divorce would be a legitimate question between two people who were dating. But it seemed a little too personal for the situation he was in with her. Time, however, was short. And he was not going to waste any of it dancing around explanations.

"That's easy. We didn't love each other anymore," he responded, taking a moment to watch her reaction. "Fact is, I'm not sure we ever loved each other the way you should to get married. You know, that 'can't live without you' love?"

"Like we had? Until we didn't?"

Callie's expression sank as her words fell off to silence.

"Yes. Like that," he confirmed quietly.

Jason could see that she was reliving the hurt from twenty-seven years ago. A hurt that should have mellowed and disappeared over time. But, obviously now, it was an injury that was still tender.

"Then why did you?" she asked, eager to know the answer but afraid of what it would imply.

"She was pregnant," he answered as he looked away, embarrassed by the comment. "We were tracking but not that close to it relationship-wise. But that pregnancy changed everything. What should have had a million reasons 'why,' like you and I had, was decided by 'why nots.'"

"That's scary."

"Tell me about it. With four daughters, I'm praying that they make the right decision regardless of their situation."

"It worked out though, right? I mean, you had a happy family?"

Callie would never have expected to feel sympathy for Jason for any reason until now. Her life, despite the rough patches and problems she was dealing with now, was genuinely happy and fun with a spouse she generally enjoyed spending time with and cherished as a loving husband and father to her children.

"You can make anything happy," Jason answered, as if he had thought it through and created a case statement on the matter. "It's easy to lose yourself in a happy family when the house is full. Just have more kids! Everything is so crazy. You don't have a moment to even think about happiness. But that changes once the kids start peeling out and you find yourself looking at each other again."

"That's so sad. So, your split was mutual?"

"I guess. We worked it out to split everything. Then she talked to a lawyer who told her all sorts of things and charged her a fortune only for her to end up with what we originally agreed on."

"That sucks for her," Callie commented, trying to throw some humor into the conversation.

"Me too," Jason answered as he finished his glass of wine. "We split his bill. But we're amicable now."

Callie smiled at the honesty and the fact that Jason took a dramatic chug of his wine before defining the final resolution of his divorce. It was obviously hard for him to talk about. But she got the sense that it was the first time he did with an ear he trusted. As he refilled his glass and offered her a top-off, it seemed necessary to finish the confession.

"Well, being amicable. That's good for your kids. Right?" she asked.

The question itself was to not just to finish Jason's story but to shed some light on the many considerations Callie had during the drive down and through their time together. Her children were her center. Her life experience included parents that stayed together and a mother who was crushed when her father died. Despite the fact that her life with Chase was dramatically different from her parents', her faith and commitment was founded in theirs, and it was difficult to think about anything other than finishing her life with Chase. Jason was slow to respond while he swirled his wine in the moonlight.

"I suppose," he replied.

It was not quite the answer she was seeking. But it was honest and worth the risk to drill deeper.

"Do your girls come here? I mean, to the beach!?"

"From your lips to God's ears. That's why I bought it," Jason confessed as he forced a smile while still focused on his wine swirl. "Only Maya so far. Although, I do have commitments from all four for Thanksgiving. We'll see. Hopefully, no boyfriends. I don't know where I'd put them. The girls will insist they sleep with them."

Jason's eyes showed disdain for the reality that his girls had become women. The truth of the matter was that his four girls were older now than he was when he was sexually active with the girls he was dating. And his relationship with his daughters was always open enough that they would feel comfortable in making the request. His only hope was that his six-foot-four-inch frame would be daunting enough for his girls' romantic interests to offer, maybe insist, on taking a pass rather than hoping for permission.

Callie watched as all those thoughts unfolded in his head and completely understood what he was thinking. It amused her that he was so protective of them when he was such a cat at the same age.

"I'm glad you're happy," she said to bring him back into the moment.

Jason smiled while moving his eyes off his glass out into the moonlit surf.

"Getting there."

The breeze increased, pushing Callie's auburn-brown hair back from her face. Despite the rain, Jason noticed she had gotten some color from the day and maybe a little windburn from the Jeep rides. He adjusted the blanket before putting his arm behind her. Her eyes closed in the comfort of his touch as he looked off into the darkness.

## 10

Jason opened his eyes to find himself still on the bench with Callie. For a moment, he thought he had dreamt the entire visit. He was happy to still find her there. As he watched her in silence, she looked up to find him back in the present.

"Penny for your thoughts?" she asked, as if the question had stood ready for minutes.

"I'm thinking about whether or not we'd be here, right now, if we married twenty-six—"

"Seven," Callie corrected.

"Twenty-SEVEN years ago," he repeated with a confirming smile and added emphasis on seven. "And, if so, what would our family be like?"

"Definitely would have had girls," she stated with raised eyebrows, remembering from high school biology that the male determined a child's sex.

"That's for sure," he replied. "But how many?"

Callie knew she did not enjoy being pregnant given the sickness, swelling, and hormonal mood swings. But she did love tending to babies and running around with little kids in tow. Three was a load of work that ended too soon, leading to her current emptiness. But four children seemed excessive, if not impossible.

"As the oven doing the baking, three was enough," she decided for them.

"I really liked four," Jason responded as if in a trance. "It was so crazy... and soooo fucking expensive. But I loved every minute of it. But the reality is for us to have had kids—"

"We wouldn't have the ones we have now," Callie finished for him. "And that's unthinkable."

The thought shocked Jason back into reality while triggering an immediate sadness in Callie about what her weekend there with Jason could do to her children. Jason had often wondered what his life and family would look like had he married Callie. His career of entrepreneurialism would have changed to a corporate track if Callie's dad had been his father-in-law. In hindsight, that may have been a better path. But Jason, like Callie, loved his kids for who they were and all the experiences he had with them. The thought of swapping out children threw another wet rag onto the fun of the evening's speculation of what could have been.

"I can't imagine any of them not in my life," he pondered out loud as he became emotional.

As he wiped the tears from his eyes, Callie thought what was happening was an odd twist of roles for them. She was usually the one that cried while he would bring her back to reality. His divorce must have taken a bigger toll on his relationships with his kids than he shared. It was now her turn to revive the happiness.

"I bet you were a great dad," she said, adding a playful punch to his chest.

"And you a great mom," he answered, smiling at the thought.

"I was," she replied proudly, then blurted. "I AM!"

For a moment she was lost in the fantasy of the what-ifs until realizing the reality of their lives with other spouses and other children born to other families.

"I can see it. I could always see it," he answered. "I'm guessing you learned how to cook?"

The question surprised Callie as it was always a button that Chase and the kids could push when they wanted to either go out or get takeout.

"No. Not really." She laughed. "But I do have a killer kitchen. I don't even know what most of it is for."

The kitchen was part of a compromise that Callie worked out with Chase when he came home unannounced with his Maserati. Although she enjoyed riding in the car with its speed and the looks it got, the leverage it provided her as an extravagant purchase opened the opportunity to get the kitchen her friends had and that she coveted. The add-on agreement to take cooking classes fell to the wayside as soon as the kitchen was installed.

"I recall a really lethal broccoli-chicken dish when we were dating," Jason said with a twinge of sarcasm.

"Really? You say that now? I was trying to impress you! GOD, you're so mean!"

Jason savored the response that livened Callie's face and ended with a slap on his chest. The slight pain did not last long enough. But the ensuing smile was what he had been seeking all day. It was an indicator to him that they were back on good terms and beyond the delicate dancing that had to happen as each renewed their understanding of the other.

"I think we would've made it," he said while leaning back onto the bench.

"I'm not so sure now." she replied, still staring at him. "Doesn't matter though. We didn't try."

Although rich in truth, *'We didn't try'* killed the conversation. Jason also knew that single summary statement was not the complete story. Callie did try. He was the one that ran. There was nothing more to talk about on the matter. They both turned to the darkness to regroup.

"I had a religion professor who said 'You'll marry the person you're with when you're ready to marry.'"

"That's pretty convenient," Callie replied, surprised by his dramatic shift in thinking. "You definitely weren't ready at twenty-eight to marry me."

"And I wasn't 'ready' at thirty-one either when I did get married," he added. "Likely never would've happened had I not been 'pushed.'"

"That's bullshit," she answered with a little anger in her voice.

"It's true. But I did it, and it worked out OK. Well, sort of."

Callie's immediate thought was that his marriage could not have been 'OK' if it lacked love throughout and ended in divorce. But his comment opened all sorts of thoughts in her head about their own failed engagement.

"So, if I hadn't given you the ring back, you would have married me?"

It was a question she had pondered many times since the night it happened.

"Without a doubt," he answered, as he turned to look her in the eyes.

"What? Why?"

His answer shook her. On the night she returned his ring, he just took it quietly without objection, then disappeared into the darkness. No words. No explanation. He just left, abandoning her, her family, and his mother to clean up the mess left behind to cancel the ceremony, the reception, and to return all the wedding presents.

Jason knew she deserved the truth and hesitated on how deep to go. So, he started with the broad strokes, hoping it would be enough to avoid the underlying finer details.

"Because, Callie, I have never loved anyone as deeply as I loved you," he confessed, releasing all the anguish that had built in him over the past twenty-seven years. "And you would've been great for me."

Callie's eyes filled with tears as each word was said.

"Then why did you take it back?" she asked quietly, not knowing if she really wanted to hear the answer.

"Because I was afraid... afraid I would be really bad for you," he answered. "Which would've hurt you more and killed us."

Jason's words turned Callie's sadness to anger. It was not what she expected. What she was hearing was that he had no faith that she could handle tough times.

"What a crock of shit!" she blurted without thinking.

"No, everything I feared came true. Life was really hard," he answered, trying to dial down her response.

"Thanks so much for giving me a no-confidence vote."

"I was protecting you."

"Bullshit!"

Jason could see his reasons were being taken as insults. His explanations were honest as to why he took the ring back and ran. He just did not know it at the time it happened. He needed Callie to see that he left her so that she could find the life she deserved and got.

"Trust me," he stated in a soft voice to calm her anger. "It got really desperate at times. I've seen your life, and it wasn't ours."

"You have no clue what my life has been," she replied, getting hotter. "And again. Thanks for having such great faith in me. I wasn't marrying you for what you could give me! I wanted to share my life with you... have children WITH YOU... LOVE YOU!"

"I'm sorry."

"This is really insulting. Who the fuck are you to protect me!?"

Callie stood as her anger continued to build. Jason's explanation was failing to answer anything. It just built more questions. Questions that if answered like the last group were going to cause more damage. She was done with him.

"You know what?" she said, calming down into tears. "I don't know why I came here. You're obviously just fucking with me."

Panicked by the remark, Jason reached to take hold of her arm as she turned to walk away.

"Wait! I'm not. Please... Just stay."

He released his grasp and let her continue a few steps until she stopped. As she turned back to him, her eyes were red and swollen with tears flowing down her sunburned cheeks.

"Why!? Why should I stay? You obviously see me as weak and unable to deal with anything heavy," she said while teetering back and forth. "I bet that's what you still see now. I can't deal with my marriage situation now, so I run to find something comfortable. Are you going to protect me now, Jason!?"

Jason watched Callie struggle with her emotions and her looming decision to leave. He knew if she left that it would be the last time he would ever see or talk to her. He had experienced that pain before and its continuous looming over him for the past twenty-seven years. His explanation did run deeper than what he shared. His fear was that more disclosure would explain things too well and end everything at that moment. He tried to buy time to think.

"That's not it at all," he answered, knowing it to be true.

"Then what!?" she replied, looking for any reason to stay.

But Jason stayed silent and still to the question.

"Fuck you, Jason Cartwright!" she screamed. "I'm out of here. MOLLY!"

Jason remained still as Callie walked off to the cottage. Zoe and Molly followed and beat her to the sliding door. As she grabbed the handle, she stopped. Motionless for a moment, she stood in place as the dogs danced by her feet. Jason followed slowly behind her, wanting, and fearful, to either reach out or say anything. She was surprised by his presence when she turned to go back.

"You know. I think it really sucks that you expect me to tell you everything right away when you bailed on me five fucking weeks before our wedding without an explanation! Tell me, Jason, how's it feel now!?"

"I honestly didn't know why I had to go," he replied with a placid face. "I just knew I had to go."

Callie watched his eyes that did not move and appeared lifeless. Jason was surrendering. He was watching her leave and likely hating him again.

"Well that's just dandy. You just disappeared. You never even said goodbye! So, let's see how you like it. And this won't even be close to what you did to me as you won't have the embarrassment I did."

Jason didn't reply as Callie angrily opened the door and disappeared into the cottage. He watched the bedroom light illuminate the hallway. Her shadow danced on the walls as she packed her clothes to make her exit. Jason's heart ached as it did on the day he heard she had committed to marry someone else. He was losing her again and with a renewed anger toward him. This would be the last time he would see her.

###

Callie's hands flew up in frustration as her suitcase tumbled down the wood stairs to the parking area. Its final resting spot was upside-down, leaning against a pillar that was driven into the sand. Jason ran to the top of the stairs as she continued her descent with Molly on lead in one hand and holding the handrail with the other. He followed them both, hoping she would stop, hoping the suitcase fall would be too much, and hoping that she would stay. But she kept forging on. She grabbed her bag out of the sand and continued to her car without looking back.

The back of the Range Rover opened automatically. She banged the suitcase wheels on the cement pad, looking for the stuck sand to release. Little fell, and like the hurt, most was going to make the ride home with her. Frustrated, she lifted and hurled her bag into the back compartment. The thud of its impact carried across the parking area as it settled into place, releasing sand she would have to sweep up later. More wounds to deal with and, hopefully, not anything for her to explain.

Callie opened the passenger door and hastily loaded Molly. Not once did she either look at Jason or speak to him. Jason knew her departure was imminent, barring anything dramatic.

"I'm self-destructive!" screamed out of his mouth without any forethought.

Callie stopped her effort to situate Molly. Confused by his outburst, she paused to think, then turned to look at him.

"What?"

Jason stepped forward, thinking that would enable her to hear better.

"I am..." he said, then paused. "I... was... self-destructive."

Callie took a deep breath to understand.

"What does that even mean?" she asked, desperate to hear something to let her stay.

"It means I intentionally destroy things after I build them. Careers, friendships, relationships. At least, I used to."

Jason felt naked with the confession that exposed his most embarrassing flaw.

Callie stood still as she thought through his words and the impact it all had on their relationship, his life, and his family's destruction. The confession itself was borderline unbelievable and would have pushed most people away. But for Callie, it filled the void in her life created by the mystery of why Jason left. It also instilled in her a desire to know more.

"I would've noticed that," she declared, in a questioning tone.

"No, you wouldn't have. I didn't even know I was doing it," he answered. "It just subtly did its thing."

"That's the most frightening thing I've ever heard."

"Frightening, toxic, incredibly selfish, and completely inexcusable," Jason finished.

"In a nutshell."

As she watched Jason rattle off each descriptive word, Callie mentally checked agreement with each of them. But there was an oddity that destructive Jason was the opposite of destructive when he wanted something. At that point, he was generous, thoughtful, warm, friendly, funny, and supportive. The Jekyll-and-Hyde personality would not have made much sense to her if not for Chase's experience helping a bipolar friend through many rough patches a few years back. She knew this was not the same thing. But its polar behavioral qualities gave Callie understanding that, back then, Jason did not know why he left her back then like he did today.

"And, It's... no more?" Callie asked, to clarify his status now.

"It's no more," he exhaled. "It ruined so much. You and me being the biggest thing. Admitting it was a huge challenge. But I'm fine now."

"Fine?" Callie questioned in disbelief. "You just ended two of the biggest parts of your life in the past two years. How are things possibly 'fine' now?"

Jason closed his eyes as he walked toward Callie. Her passenger door was still open with Molly in the seat eager to get going. He stopped to gather his thoughts. As he opened his eyes, he saw a look of compassion on her face that showed she was listening even if not yet believing.

"I know. It doesn't make sense," he opened. "But both were good events for me. My business helped me work through and fix the issues. It was a marketing business, project-based, with a beginning, an end and, best of all, constant newness. We got people to notice, like, and want our client's stuff. Our secret sauce was creating the silent lure to get people to want the client product instead of advertising it to them."

"Like on TV shows, movies."

Callie's experience in advertising gave her an understanding of brand placements.

"YES. Social media influencers, you name it," Jason added to fill in the rest. "The project stream kept me engaged. The lifesaver was hiring and trusting managers to build the business. Otherwise, I would have sold it way too soon. Through all that, I really got to understand 'me.' I only sold the company to give Steph her half in cash, and the offer was generous."

Callie stayed silent, waiting for more that better related to her than to Jason's work. He took a deep breath to continue while looking again to see if she still wanted to hear his story. Her focus and expression were not changing. He took one last moment to collect his thoughts, then started.

"My divorce was a different story. It could've ended after Rachel or when the kids were young. But the family kept evolving. It was very chaotic, fun, and, most of all, distracting. These were my children that I wanted to spend every moment possible with. I got involved in their schools, sports, and drove them all over the place just for the time together. It was fantastic and not worth trading for anything. I think Steph would say the same thing. But that all ended as they started to go to college. When Maya left, Stephanie was the one who asked for the divorce. Although, she'd been hinting at it for years."

"I don't see that as a failure. It's just sad," Callie responded. "You stayed committed to it. That says a lot."

"Yes... and no. It didn't have the love it should have had. As Steph would say, we were just good friends raising kids."

"So, you saw you and me getting married as an end?"

"It sounds so stupid. But yes. An end to independence rather than the beginning of something bigger and better than my wildest imagination. My life with Steph and the kids showed me all of that for the win of just the family experience."

"Me being here must be really fucking with your head," Callie stated apologetically.

Jason laughed at her continued use of the F word. But that was Callie when she got mad. When they were younger, it was even funnier when the refined little girl he loved would go on a tirade of F-bombs when pissed off. And this time, it was the perfect word. No other verb would have filled the descriptor that Callie had just captured. Even if she was wrong.

"It's actually been really healthy," he answered, giving her relief. "Believe me. You being here clears up a lot of things and feelings for me... So... Please stay? There's more to say. And, if not for that, stay because it's late, and you've been drinking."

Callie's earlier rage had subsided during the time and confessions that had just happened. A few minutes earlier, she could have driven right over Jason and left him for dead in the street. But, with the revelation just presented, she saw the usually highly confident man that earlier stood before her for who he truly was. The wounds from his actions of twenty-plus years ago were still raw to the touch. But now, her understanding of the reasons for his actions encouraged her to stay to learn more. She had no idea where anything was heading. But she wanted to complete the journey she started.

# # #

Jason placed Callie's suitcase next to the sliding glass door as Molly and Zoe headed down the walkway to the beach. The night was still clear with the cool onshore breeze. They returned to their seats on the bench and wrapped the blanket that was there around them. Jason refilled Callie's glass with Merlot, then emptied the rest of the bottle into his glass. They both took immediate drinks to calm their nerves and to think about their next topic of conversation.

"I'm still processing what you said."

Callie was not interested in letting the confessions go. Jason expected continued questions, having gone through the same conversation with Stephanie throughout their marriage. It was Stephanie who first identified the issue after Jason quickly sold an emerging small company of great promise to invest in a startup that did not work. During a heated exchange, her question of why he was so self-destructive stuck with them both, making the final diagnosis possible.

"I hope, in the end, you'll understand and forgive me," he answered, uncertain of Callie's view of him.

"If I hadn't forgiven you already, I wouldn't be here," she replied. "But it is weirdly comforting to know why things happened as they did."

"I just look back on decisions in my life and think 'what the fuck?' I mean, I destroyed so many great things that should've been."

"So, what now?" she asked, thinking *he's free and has the opportunity to do whatever he wants.*

"This is it."

"You'll get bored with this. Or lonely. Do you think you will marry again?"

"Maybe... Bored, that is." He smiled at the qualification. "And no. I'm not going to marry again. After being told I was a shitty husband for fifteen years, I think I'll spare the world that."

Callie felt a sadness for him. The man that she knew long ago combined with the man sitting with her now should share his life and happiness with someone.

"You were just with the wrong person," she reasoned, trying to add perspective. "You can't live the rest of your life alone."

"I hope not to."

"Well, good luck with that if you're not willing to commit."

"I'll commit with everything I have and can give. The married thing just makes it too... contractual..."

Jason thought he had found the right word, then looked to Callie for approval she did not give.

"Would you marry again?" he asked.

"I'm married now."

"Yet, you're here."

"Here we go again," she responded, throwing her hands up and pulling away from him. "I just came here to see you."

"That's all?"

Callie felt all the forgiveness she had for Jason bleed out of her with his question. She tossed her remaining wine over the rail onto the sand and stood.

"You know what? I'm not doing this again."

"I'm just asking an honest question," Jason implored. "I told you mine; tell me yours... please."

"OH MY GOD. You're such an asshole!"

Jason grabbed hold of Callie's arm as he watched her anger reappear. Tethering her in place seemed to be his only option to keep her from storming out again.

"I'm sorry," he said sincerely. "I just want to know."

The tense resistance he felt when taking hold relaxed. Her stature dropped from stiff to huddled as tears of emotion replaced her fit of anger. A barrier had been broken.

"That's not why I'm here," she responded while pulling out of Jason's releasing grasp. "I've been married for almost twenty-five years to the same man and have three children. I freely and openly made a commitment to God, my parents, my family, and TO MY HUSBAND to love him until I die. MY GOD! I have a daughter to marry, boys, grandchildren someday. How can I do all of that without their father? What would that look like?"

"Who cares what it looks like?" Jason replied, having just lived through all of her considerations to find his own freedom and happiness. And to give his ex-wife hers.

"I care. It's important to me," she answered.

"Then why are you here?" he asked, knowing the potential for the question to flash back into his face.

"You said it didn't matter."

Callie turned toward the water and took hold of the railing. Her head sank as her eyes closed, releasing a wash of tears over her cheeks. Jason walked behind her and placed his hands on her shoulders for comfort. He knew Callie had to honestly address her purpose for being with him to decide on the direction for the rest of her life.

"Just be honest," he said. "I promise. You'll feel better."

"I didn't..." She struggled. "I didn't... I was curious. I honestly thought I'd chicken out when I saw you... If I saw you. But I didn't. I had the chance to let you pull away. And, I didn't. I actually ran to stop you."

Jason felt a warmth run through his soul as Callie finished her confession. It was a scenario he'd played out in his head for decades and one that he had convinced himself would never happen.

"I'm really happy you did," he said, turning her around to face him. "Look, this is really unfair to tell you now, but there hasn't been one day go by SINCE WE MET... IN THAT STUPID BUFFET LINE, and particularly since our engagement broke, that I haven't thought of you."

Callie cried as he finished his confession.

"Oh my God, Jason. That is really unfair to say."

"You've been constantly in my head. Where you are. What you're doing. Who you're with."

"I've wondered the same things sometimes too," she answered, looking back at him.

Jason smiled as Callie confirmed that he had not been forgotten. Given how things ended between them, he just assumed he became a bad memory packed into her mind with a special lock never to be opened.

"I would've loved that craziness with you," he said while visualizing a picture of his words. "You, pregnant, with swollen feet blows my mind to think about. A gaggle of kids in the grocery store, a restaurant, makes me smile every time. Fact is, I wanted to reconnect with you up until you got married. But I couldn't keep putting you through my insanity, hoping for it to work when it never did. That's assuming you would have even given me a chance. So, I let go... and moved away so you could find your 'one.'"

His last word brought Callie back to real time. The fantasy was warming for her to think about. But the reality still existed.

"And I did find my 'one,'" she answered. "And I am still married to him. And I do love him. He's the father of my children."

Jason felt slippage as he watched her face shift from emotional to practical.

"I'm not debating anything here," he replied. "That's as it should be."

There was a level of honor being maintained in Jason's approach to Callie's thought process. He was keenly aware that she was fragile and likely could be romanced and manipulated. But she was hurting. His goal, therefore, was for her to process everything completely for herself and her life to the likely impacts a decision to either stay with him or to go back home would have on her over the long term. A weekend triumph was not his strategy.

"I appreciate you saying that, but I'm here now... with you," Callie stated, appearing to ease her conscience through each word. "I don't feel bad for being here, or ashamed. I feel quite 'right' for a change."

Her words shook Jason's soul. It was a long-standing dream becoming real before him when he could mend his mistakes from the past without destroying his family and his world. That realization also created guilt within him when he remembered that Callie's situation was not the same as his. Still, he was happy to hear her words.

"I don't know what to tell you," he replied with a soft smile. "I'm just really glad to see you and to hear your voice again."

Callie responded with an unsure smile as he wrapped his arms around her and pulled her close. She relaxed in his hold without returning the normal tight grasp she liked to give. He kissed her on the top of her head as a comfort as much for him as it was for her.

After waiting a few moments, Callie tried to release from him. Jason continued to hold on until her soft push to separate became something he couldn't ignore. She turned back toward the bench while wiping her eyes on her shirt sleeve. The drama of the conversation and the confessions were over. Callie returned to her seat and took a drink from Jason's wine glass. He sat next to her, thinking about how to finish their talk.

"I'm so glad to finally have told you everything. It's been pressure cooking in me for decades. I have owed you an explanation and an honest apology for all the shit I put you through... I just didn't know how, or even if you cared."

Callie remained still and just looked at him in silence. The conversation exhausted her emotionally and mentally.

"I'm glad you told me," she finally answered. "I never knew why we just fell apart."

"I'm truly sorry for all of it, and regret everything. It's so hard to live life when you had everything and threw it away."

"I don't know what to say," she answered, still holding his wine glass.

Jason's eyes were red and teary as he thought about the decades lost with her. Although the conversation was healthy for them, it was also exhausting. He had confessed and apologized for the sins he had made that split them to be with other people. The pain of that loss haunted him and appeared to be still unresolved to haunt him again.

"How about nothing?" he answered. "I don't deserve any sympathy or comfort."

Jason looked away with that suggestion as Callie watched and studied his response. The conversation stayed quiet for several minutes as they both turned their attention back to the waves illuminated by the streak of moon-glow that washed over them. Callie knew Jason was in another place, likely running thoughts through his head about them as a couple and as parents. His face remained still and stoic. She waited for him to return to her to finish their evening. A finish she knew would be respectful to her marriage and life situation.

As she readjusted her body on the bench for comfort, Jason tuned back into them, surprised he'd been 'gone' for the moment.

"Wow," he opened, looking to shake lingering thoughts out of his head. "You know what? I think we've had enough honesty to think about. Let's get you situated for tonight and see what tomorrow brings."

Callie agreed and was happy to change locations to where she could be alone to compile all the events of the day. Together they stood and walked back to the cottage. Jason's focus was on picking up all the items around them. Callie's thinking was more concerned about what bedtime would bring.

## 11

Jason exited the bathroom and returned to his room to change for bed. Normally, he would just pile in wearing underwear and a fresh t-shirt. But Callie's presence demanded more decorum, which he accommodated by adding running shorts. It felt weird, but appropriate, that he was adding layers to his sleepwear when, as a couple, they would have been helping the other to shed them.

Callie waited until Jason's door closed before heading into the bathroom. Still processing everything from the day and on autopilot with his bedtime routine, Jason returned to find the bathroom door closed. While waiting, he heard the toilet flush. As Callie opened the door to head back to her room, she stopped just short of running into him as he stood there in his bewilderment.

"This is weird," he said with a squirrelly look on his face.

Callie felt an immediate pressure build within her. She trusted him by staying. She was unsure if his presence in the hallway was meant to suggest anything.

"I'm not going to say I haven't thought about it today…. I can't even say I don't want to… But I can't. Not with everything…"

Jason smiled and held up his hand.

"Stop. I wasn't looking for you to offer. And I'm not asking. It's also been so long I'm not so sure everything works, anyway."

Callie smiled at the confession and wondered if there was any truth to his lack of activity. It did, however, refresh her spirit to hear his words and, even more so, to think that he had gone without sex for a long period of time. A revelation she found perversely gratifying. But she also knew she initiated their first sensual touch, which she did not regret, but should not have let happened.

"That kiss shouldn't have happened," she admitted. "That was unfair. I'm sorry."

Jason understood that she was setting boundaries in the conversation that he never intended to cross, regardless of how the day ended.

"That kiss was innocent and wonderful," he said with a reassuring smile to show it was appreciated and enjoyed.

To calm her anxiety, Jason extended his arms out to invite a hug.

"Friend hug?" he asked, in a joking tone.

Callie smiled as her shoulders dropped from their rigid, defensive posture. She took his hands in hers, then toed-up to give him another slow, light kiss on the mouth. She then hugged him tightly, inflicting that wonderful pain again. As she let go, she looked at his crotch and smiled.

"Good news," she said, as she patted him on the chest. "It all still works."

Jason responded with a sad smile as he took a step back. Although his motor was running and she was right in front of him, he was not looking for anything beyond an anxious night of no-sleep because she was in bed next door to him. Callie touched his arm, then turned to her room.

"Good night, Jason," she said softly as she reached for the door.

As Callie entered the guestroom, Molly recognized that her opportunity to sleep with Callie would close with the door. She ran into the room and jumped onto the bed to be sleeping partner. Jason, in turn, headed into his room with Zoe, who took her usual spot at the bottom of his bed.

#

The room was quiet and more enclosed than what Callie was used to either at home or when vacationing in Nantucket. The mattress was new and comfortable. The sheets were Egyptian cotton and at least 5000 thread-count. The simple décor and appointments were for comfort. Callie settled in with her bedside lamp lit and Molly by her side.

It surprised and worried Callie to realize that until now she had not thought to check her phone. The device that was her constant connector to everything was now likely filled with over a hundred unwanted emails, texts, and a few phone messages. As her phone opened to a picture of her children, she saw missed calls from Lizzie and Chase. Knowing she wasn't in the right frame of mind to talk to either of them, she chose the easier of the two to text.

sorry. lost track of time. Call tomorrow

she keyed in quickly to Lizzie, then hit send.

Immediately her screen lit with a reply. The quick response did not surprise her. Lizzie lived on her phone.

that's fine. its nice to be forgotten

Callie then took a long look at Chase's voice mail notification and decided not to listen to it. Its written translation was garbled, giving no sense of what he said. She keyed in a text to acknowledge receipt.

I'll contact you tomorrow. Going to bed.

Callie placed her phone on the nightstand, not wanting to look at any other notifications. There was likely something from Sandy too either asking or promoting the visit Callie had adamantly declared she had no interest in making. Callie thought of Sandy's face if she were to learn that not only had Callie made the journey she had suggested, but also stayed overnight at Jason's beachfront cottage. She also knew she could never share that she either kissed him or got his tent to post, as funny as that would be to the two of them.

As Callie settled from the panic of that thought, her phone pinged and lit with a text notification. She ignored it, knowing its source. She turned her light off before curling into a fetal position to sleep.

# # #

Callie's late response to his voicemail surprised Chase. Although he long ago accepted the fact that she was likely still very angry and not going to immediately respond, the late hour was long after Carolyn would have gone to bed, leaving Callie with few options beyond watching something on Netflix.

Chase's day of brotherhood included the necessary thirty-six holes of golf, a gluttonous dinner, and more alcohol than he would consume at any other time during the year. And, as far as he knew, his watchdog for overindulging in food and booze was at her mom's.

As he sat alone, having outlasted his brothers who were all passed out around the villa, Chase was being kept awake by the influence of guilt even though he was legally drunk by any standard. And Callie's message bugged him. Looking for something to do, Chase opened his *Find-my-Phone* app that he loaded on all the family cell phones when the kids first started losing theirs and then started to drive.

When the locations of the family phones loaded, it surprised him to find Callie's at the beach instead of in Williamsburg. Looking at the clock that read 1 a.m., he realized it was too late to call either her or any of his family who might be able to tell him why her phone was there and not two hours away at her mom's.

# # #

Jason knew that sleep was not going to come easy. His excitement at having Callie there and all the natural desires that came with it made falling asleep impossible. For once, he regretted not having a TV in his room to fill the time. But its noise would have penetrated the thin walls between them to disturb Callie, who was now quiet and likely asleep from the exhaustion of the day.

Zoe was in her usual spot, sprawled out at his feet, asleep, and snoring. Jason turned off his bedside lamp then laid on his back, hoping to find some way to fall asleep. It did not work. His mind was running with too many thoughts as his eyes fixated on the rotating fan that was lit by the moonglow that leaked through his window shades.

As Jason rolled to his side to face the door, he heard a jostle in the hallway that he assumed to be Callie heading to the bathroom. As he stayed still to listen, his door opened slowly as she entered with a blanket wrapped around her. Saying nothing, she laid down on his bed to face the wall. As she settled, she slowly backed toward him as if seeking a place to nest. Puzzled, Jason stayed as he was until she reached back for his arm to pull over her. He then slid closer to where she wanted him to be, took a deep breath she could feel, then closed his eyes. They both fell asleep almost instantly.

## 12

The rays from the morning sun illuminated the steam that rose from the asphalt parking lot. Although it was October, the temperatures in Raleigh stayed in the mid-eighties and the remaining moisture from the week's rain when combined with the sun's heat still created a steamy fog.

Maya Cartwright never missed an opportunity to make the journey from NC State to the Outer Banks to spend a day or so at the beach with her dad. She knew that despite the fantasy island environment he had chosen with the new friends he had found, he was lonely. She quickly loaded her overnight bag along with a backpack full of the books and the computer she had no intention of looking at into her Mini Cooper convertible.

The Wolfpack red Mini was a surprise from her dad after doing well her freshman year in school. She also knew divorce guilt motivated it. But that was never discussed. Each of her sisters had cars in school that were more traditional. So, Maya was not going to complain. The North Carolina weather, along with her new place to stay at the beach whenever she wanted, made the convertible a highly desirable win for her.

Maya hit the road with the roof down. The early morning sun was in her face to be taken out by an old pair of Persol Calligrapher sunglasses that were once her dad's. Her auburn hair flowed in the wind as she shifted through the gears to surpass the posted speed limit on the interstate.

Before she left, Maya took a moment to tune in her favorite Spotify playlist titled *Songs when driving with Dad*. It was a selection of tunes they both liked, that had no swear words, and that was developed and refined over years of driving to club soccer tournaments while Maya was in high school.

The two hundred mile drive that Google maps said should take three hours typically took just over than two and a half to complete. She expected her dad to be up and about when she arrived.

# # #

Sunlight replaced the moonlight that had crept into the master bedroom the night before. After settling in with Jason, Callie slept heavy and was fully relaxed when she woke. Those two feel-goods were contrary to any expectation she had thought possible at any point the night before.

Callie woke to find herself still wrapped in the cotton blanket she brought with her from the guest bedroom. It was to be her security in the event she was wrong about her ex-lover's honor and expectations. Their night together was not unlike others she remembered from their past. They shared a bed well, and her sleep was secure and uninterrupted.

As Callie tuned in to her surroundings, she felt an immediate urge to visit the bathroom. The wine had processed through her body and was pressing on her bladder for release. But, as she moved to sit up, she found her blanket weighted down from behind.

Callie did not want to wake Jason just to go to the bathroom; but the situation was becoming urgent. As she tugged to get free, a grumble came from behind her as dead weight began to shift into her back and further onto her blanket.

The time soon came when there was no choice but to take drastic action to get to the bathroom. As she pulled harder on the blanket, it released allowing her to sit up to head for relief. As she looked back to see if she woke him, the dead weight pinning her down wagged her tail and gave a good morning smile. Jason was gone. Zoe had assumed his spot next to Callie in his bed.

Seeing Jason gone surprised her. Callie was a light sleeper and should have heard him leave. As she exited the bathroom, she started toward the living room listening for sounds of life. But the house was still and silent outside of the two dogs looking to her to let them out.

As she walked into the living room wearing the same silk pajamas she wore at her mother's, she remembered Jason's addiction to the Sunday morning political talk shows. That was a common thread he shared with Chase. Although Jason only watched for sport, Chase did it for work. Those talk shows were one of the things over the years that would make Callie think of Jason on Sunday mornings while her husband was in the room.

As she walked into the living room, Callie expected to see the oversized TV lit with Jason slumped on the couch. It surprised her when she found the room empty and the TV off. Wondering where he could be, she wandered into the kitchen to check the coffee maker. There was a comforting smell that said really good coffee was hot and waiting for her. A mug that said *Raddest Dad* sat next to the carafe. She decided to start her day with a mug of Jason's finest brew.

The coffee steamed as she added half-n-half and sweetener. She relaxed as she swallowed her first taste and looked around the living space once again. The cottage was now comfortable to her.

The dogs scampered about her feet while she went from room to room then outside both looking for Jason and to confirm that he was for real instead of just part of a bizarre dream.

As Callie closed the sliding door, the two dogs immediately darted for the end of the walkway. She took a quick look under the house for the Jeep that was still there. Her first thought was that he was on a run for the pastries she saw at the coffee shop. But the coffee shop was over a mile away and a place he would have to drive to.

As Callie studied the larger houses around her, she admired Jason's cottage exterior with new appreciation. Shabby-chic fit him better than what his neighbors had constructed. However, the cleanliness of a pool with its lack of aquatic life both large and small would be an improvement she would choose for his home.

The dogs were gathered at the closed gate, eager to hit the beach. As Callie approached, she continued to study the dunes and seascape looking for Jason. Callie let the dogs go who immediately squatted to pee as soon as they hit the sand. Callie smiled as she watched them begin their game of endless circling, while also wondering why Jason was nowhere to be found.

As she watched the two dogs play closer to the water, her eyes shifted from the sand to the surf. She noticed a figure out beyond the waves slowly moving horizontally to the shoreline. It reminded her of watching the lifeguards in Nantucket who trained by swimming parallel to shore while pulling a life-saving floatation bullet behind them. The swimmer she was watching had the same trailer. She watched him, or her, for a moment, then checked the shoreline again for Jason.

Callie was about halfway through her mug of coffee when she scanned back across the waterfront. Zoe and Molly were knee deep in the surf barking at the swimmer who was now sitting upright in the water. As she focused on his face, she realized that the swimmer she saw a few moments earlier was also the same person she had been looking for. Jason watched as she tuned-in, He started waving as soon as she leaned forward to confirm her sighting.

"You're such a nerd," she whispered to herself as she returned his wave.

Happy that she saw him, Jason declared his swim was over and rolled back into the water. As he went under, he released the life-saving bullet that popped out of the water into the air. He finished his swim bodysurfing to the shoreline.

Parking near the coffee shop was not the challenge it tended to be in the summer and early fall. High season brought in the vacationers, who were easily identified by minivans with toppers and Suburbans with toppers and bike racks. Arriving after 10 a.m. in the summertime risked that available parking would be a lot or two over, and that all the pastries would be gone. But Maya was now a regular, having made several fall trips to visit her dad. Some were planned in advance. Others, Maya would just show up. Regardless of the advance warning, Jason was always happy to see his youngest daughter along with any college friend she would bring to visit.

The pastry racks were half-full as Maya joined the short line of patrons waiting to order their morning brew and favorite treats. She found the lemon poppyseed muffins that were her dad's favorite and added a few glazed doughnuts and others to create a dozen that would last him well into the week.

Maya loved time at the beach. It proved to be the perfect resurrection environment for her relationship with her dad after the divorce that she and her sisters had seen coming. Her expectation was that Jason would be somewhere in his swim when she arrived. She hoped to surprise him as he returned from the water to enjoy his Sunday morning coffee and political TV shows. She placed the box of sweets securely on her front passenger seat. After inhaling a deep draw of the fresh sea air, Maya started the last mile to his cottage.

#

As Jason stood to leave the water, an unexpected wave hit him from behind. Its force pushed him sideways, causing him to stumble and to fall into the shallow water. Embarrassed, he looked to see if Callie was watching. A toast of her coffee mug confirmed his fear. *Raddest Dad* had to recompose his cool.

As he walked shirtless from the surf, Callie studied the physique that until then had been covered in cloth. Although thin, his build was still soft and looked more like a man of his age than the young twenty-something she remembered. She watched as he shook his towel in the wind to rid it of sand to dry off. As he made his way toward her, he covered up with a Virginia Cavaliers t-shirt given to him on Father's Day by his daughter Faith. The dogs followed.

"I'm impressed," Callie stated as he emerged into sight at the top of the stairs.

"Don't be. I use these, and rely on this, to take breaks," Jason replied while lifting his shortened flippers and foam bullet. "So, I cheat."

"Still pretty dang impressive," she responded. "My husband won't even go into the water."

Jason made one more pass over his hair with his towel to ensure it was dry. He then finger-combed it into place, hoping it looked OK and did not have any alfalfa shafts spiking anywhere.

"Yeah, well, when I got here I wouldn't go in the water either," he admitted. "I was heavier. It wasn't pretty."

Callie smiled at the confession.

"I heard," she stated, using her mug to shield her amusement.

"Rebecca?"

"Rebecca," she confirmed, knowing Rebecca would find it funny to know she put Jason in an awkward spot.

Jason was eager to move on from their physique conversation. Getting heavy was the result of several colliding forces in his life. He was proud of the fact that he had committed to a regimen that resulted in the loss of weight he wanted without complete sacrifice of all the great foods and drinks life at the beach offered. As Callie finished another sip of coffee, Jason pointed to her mug.

"Did you, by chance, bring me one?"

"Nope. I'm sorry," she answered, with a touch of guilt blended with a twinge of glee. "Is that my job?"

Jason frowned at the thought that he had to walk back to the cottage to get his own coffee. However, he liked the fact that Callie made her miss sound like part of a routine of an everyday visitor.

"I'll be back," he replied, as he turned to make his way back to the cottage. "What do you need?"

Callie was surprised by the question and felt she had to give an immediate, smart answer.

"I've got everything I need right here," she declared quickly, grimacing at the realization the context of her answer was not quite what she intended to say.

Jason smiled as he walked away. He hoped there was some truth in her slip.

"Alright then!" he shouted into the air as he turned to walk backwards to the cottage. "As of right now, your status has changed from guest to family. You have to grab what you want, when you want it. Don't be shy."

Callie's chest tightened with each word. She knew what he meant as well as what he intended for her to hear. She raised her eyebrows and smiled as she took another pull of coffee.

## 13

The carafe of coffee was still hot to the touch as Jason filled his mug. His normal routine was to have coffee first, swim, then finish with a banana smoothie. He found that smoothies were filling and cold enough to refresh him until lunch. With Callie present, he decided that he would get his swim done first to have coffee with her after. The meal could create itself either through him making something or them heading out to the coffee shop.

Jason filled his mug complete with a generous splash of half-n-half and two pink packs of sweetener. He returned the half-n-half to the refrigerator, wiped up the drips that were on the granite countertop, then headed back out to be with Callie. The dogs, who had gone into the cottage hoping to get something too, followed him back outside. They ran ahead to the bench where Callie was sitting. Focused on the water. Deep in thought.

# # #

It surprised Maya to see a car in her parking spot when she started her approach to her dad's property. There was just enough distance between the house and the street that two cars could park end-to-end if perpendicular to the road. Maya's speed and last-minute realization did not put her in a good position to gracefully park behind either car. She skidded to a stop behind Callie's Range Rover.

As her car ended its slide across the sand-covered cement, the box of pastries she had placed on the front seat lunged forward. Her last-minute grab just as they were about to plummet from seat-top to the floor saved them.

Maya took a moment to compose herself from the unexpected excitement. She noticed the familiar Range Rover parked in her spot and was surprised to see it. Its white Virginia license plate, however, caught her eye resulting in a puzzled look. After a moment of further thought, her surprise turned to contentment. She took hold of her coffee and the box of pastries to go find her dad. The Jeep was there.

Jason could see that Callie was lost in deep thought as he approached her quietly from behind. He felt he could have fired a shotgun from where he stood, and she would not have flinched. The happy, joking persona he had left just moments earlier was gone. Her mood was serious. He was not anxious to learn why.

"Whatcha thinking about?" he asked as he nested in beside her.

"Nothing," Callie answered, comfortable with his touch but seeming separated.

"I feel a *but* coming."

Callie looked to her feet that were resting up on the bench.

"I feel guilty," she confessed.

Jason put his arm around her to comfort her as Maya walked through the living room.

"What do you have to feel guilty about? You were left alone for the weekend to find your own fun. So, you did."

"We slept together," she whispered, as if embarrassed she might be heard.

"You don't have to whisper," he whispered back before starting to laugh.

Maya noticed her dad cuddled up with someone on the bench. From the distance, the limited view of them had Maya's brain sorting through her initial thought to the possibilities from the summer and his past. As she created her list of mental finalists, it became apparent who the person was. She quietly opened the sliding door to 'catch' them.

"Can you be serious about this?" Callie asked, as she lightly smacked Jason's chest and leaned into him. "It could have..."

Maya watched the playful banter between the two as she approached. She was happy to see them both engaged and laughing together. As she got nearer, Zoe saw her coming, stood, and ran to greet her. Molly followed. Jason noticed to dogs leave knowing it meant someone unexpected had arrived.

"Mom? Dad?" Maya asked, surprised to think her parents had made peace after their amicably brutal divorce.

Jason's eyes shut with the realization that Maya had arrived unannounced and quickly stood to greet her. Callie, hearing the word 'Mom' from an unfamiliar voice, sensed an oncoming awkwardness and immediately began to slouch down on the bench while grabbing Jason's towel for cover.

"Dad?" Maya asked while walking past him to get a better look at the woman on the bench. "Is that Mom?"

Jason made it about twenty feet up the walkway. He reached out to hug his youngest daughter only to turn with her as she whisked past him without even a touch.

"Hey, sweetie," he said, while trying to remove the panic from his voice. "I'm surprised you're here."

"So I see," she replied, with her eyes locked on the top of Callie's head that had slinked lower into the bench and under the towel.

As Maya approached, Callie slowly pulled the towel from around her face to greet Jason's youngest daughter. Maya's initial look of excitement vanished with the realization that the woman on the bench was not her mother.

"Hi, I'm—" Maya started.

"Maya," Jason interjected, as both Maya and Callie looked at him, both annoyed by his habit of finishing sentences.

Maya then looked back at Callie as she set the towel aside to stand.

"Hi, Maya," Callie offered. "I'm—"

"Callie," Jason interjected again. "She's Callie."

Jason stood nervously in place as Callie and Maya both watched him nod his head up and down in affirmation of who Callie was. Maya relaxed despite her disappointment that the woman on the bench at the beach was not her mother.

In retrospect, Maya knew a reunion between her parents was an unthinkable hope that was never going to happen. She loved her parents together. However, she did not miss all the arguing that would erupt out of what should have been nothing. It was better for everyone that they were no longer together. The Virginia license plates should have been the telltale.

"Thanks, Dad. I think we could've introduced ourselves," Maya stated, in a sour tone familiar to Callie from her own daughter Lizzie. "From our call this week, I thought you'd be alone. That I'd come visit."

Jason's anxiety was spiking as he processed all the implications of Maya being there. Her presence was a wrench into his unscheduled weekend. But he also knew that once the weather turned colder, her visits to the cottage would be less frequent. Sending her back to school did not seem appropriate after her two-plus hour drive down to surprise him. He was stuck.

"I'm glad you're here," he stated matter-of-factly to reassure his daughter.

"I'm not so sure I believe you," she answered. "I'm sorry. I should've let you know."

Maya turned to return to the house. Jason knew her mindset was a fast departure back to school. He had a millisecond to decide what to do and instinctively grabbed her arm to stop her.

"Where ya going?" he asked casually to take pressure off the moment.

"Back to school," she replied.

"But that's three hours."

"For you maybe," she answered, drawing a smile from Callie. "I can go."

"No, wait," Callie inserted. "Stay. I was just getting ready to get on the road."

"What?"

Maya noticed Jason's quick and startled response to Callie's declaration. She then looked at Callie's silk attire, reaffirming her initial thought that she was intruding.

"You're in pajamas," Maya declared, looking at her from head to toe. "REALLY NICE pajamas."

Callie knew she was being called on her statement of getting ready to hit the road. She would have expected nothing less from Lizzie until she realized that the entire situation would have sent Lizzie into an epic meltdown. Having no explanation except what first came to mind, Callie looked to Jason who was thinking the same thing.

"Williamsburg," they said in unison, as if rehearsed, then smiled.

"Inside joke, I'm sure," Maya replied, somewhat embarrassed by the giddy moment. "I left doughnuts in the kitchen."

Jason again reached to take Maya's arm to keep her from leaving. He was growing comfortable with the idea of her being there as a chaperone to help keep Callie's guilt in check.

Maya's stays usually involved sitting on the beach, reading, and taking walks. She knew the Abbies as well as he did and was never hesitant to come and go as she wanted. Therefore, although first thought of as an unwelcomed surprise, Jason now saw Maya's presence as a good thing to have through the rest of the weekend.

"Doughnuts. Always a fan favorite. Thanks, sweetie," Jason said, hoping to ease Maya back into staying. "Listen. Don't go. Stay. Both of you. We've got the room."

Callie, thankful this conversation was Jason's to have with his daughter rather than hers to have with Lizzie, listened to the words and watched the mental debate go on in his head. Maya, initially, was a very untimely surprise. But, as she thought through all the implications for her, she decided that Maya's presence was a Godsend to keep things from getting out of hand. Assuming, of course, she decided to stay.

"How about," Callie interjected, "I go change for the day and let you two talk?"

She then walked to the cottage without waiting for a response. As she left, she touched Jason's arm to give him reassurance for his decision to suggest Maya stay. Maya's decision, however, had not been made.

Jason responded to her touch with a forced smile and show of concern on his brow. He waited for Callie to close the sliding door behind her to both give himself time to think and to make sure she could not hear anything that was said. When he tuned back to Maya, he found her waiting for his explanation.

"I didn't think you were coming," he said, exasperated by the happening.

"I was trying to surprise you," Maya replied quickly, as if having the response teed up to guilt him. "And when do I ever call? I thought that was Mom! Almost had a heart attack. Particularly since she has the exact-same mothership Range Rover."

Jason laughed at the comment. He had the same thought when he saw Callie's car. From the model to the color, Callie's Range Rover was identical to Stephanie's. It was her first purchase with the proceeds from the divorce. Up until that time, she was happy to drive a dressed-up Toyota Sequoia.

"The Virginia plates were what I couldn't figure out," Maya added. "I think Mom would've told me if she'd moved."

Jason loved Maya's sense of humor because it mirrored his. He pulled her in for a light hug that Callie watched from the darkness of the hallway. Satisfied that the tension between father and daughter had been resolved, she turned to get changed for the day.

"Are you OK with this?" Jason asked to reassure himself.

"What? You're going to be a monk for the rest of your life?" Maya answered, knowing the sexual insinuation would make him uncomfortable. "I can't say I'm happy with you replacing Mom and will be doing handstands later, but I'm 'OK' with you having girlfriends."

Jason felt his anxiety release as he looked with adoration toward his daughter. Despite that his ex-wife had been dating for months, this was his first experience with one of his daughters finding him with someone new. He expected it to be awkward. And it was.

"Funny you should say girlfriend... She's not my—"

"Dad, please. I don't need details," Maya replied, insinuating a one-night stand. "I can go."

"No," he insisted. "You're here. So, stay. There ARE three bedrooms."

Jason pulled Maya along with him as he started back to the house.

"I'll be in the way. It'll be awkward. I don't want to cramp your style."

Maya's decision to go back to school appeared to be final as she gave him a look of disbelief. Jason knew he just bought some time through breakfast to convince her to stay.

"Sweetie, it's fine," he answered whimsically. "Besides, I ain't got no style to cramp."

"That's a double negative. You're telling me to leave," she replied, waiting for his hold to tighten.

"No. Really. I want you to stay," he answered, as he tightened his arm around his youngest daughter. "She's just a friend. Nothing else."

## 14

Callie stirred the eggs in the pan with one hand while flipping the bacon that was resting on a paper towel next to the cooktop with the other. She looked up to see Jason attentively putting placemats onto his dining table followed by a knife, fork, and folded napkin for each setting. He had a happiness about him that she appreciated even while she felt guilty for creating the rift with Maya. She was growing concerned that Jason had become unaware that her being there was still a fantasy instead of reality. A fantasy that would be easier to resolve by waking up in Williamsburg to a crazy dream rather than dealing with the inevitable decision point she knew was coming.

Maya was outside on the deck carrying beach chairs to the end of the walkway. Zoe and Molly played on the platform, often interfering with her progress back and forth. Callie watched Maya navigate the craziness at her feet while carrying the clumsy chairs. She appeared to flow with and through what was around her, not letting it get in her way.

"She's you," Callie observed, while watching Maya dodge through the dog craziness.

Jason stopped setting the table to see what generated the comment.

"What makes you say that?" he asked.

"I don't know," she replied softly, as she moved the eggs onto a platter. "Just her vibe."

Jason was intrigued by the comment. It was the same observation many friends and family had said to him before. Maya even admitted it when aligning parent personalities with each of her siblings. He always took it as a compliment because she was successful at all the things she tried. He was also concerned that in the grand scheme of his personality, there was that single self-destructive trait he hoped ended its genetic run with him. Sadness came over him as Maya and the dogs entered through the slider. He could read it on her face. He knew her decision to return to school today was likely final.

"I put the doughnuts over there," Maya said, pointing to the box on the counter.

"Found them," Jason answered. "I've got one reserved for me."

"Of course you do," she replied snidely. "Can I help?"

"Nope. I think I've got it," Callie answered as she picked up the platter of eggs and bacon.

As expected, Jason's first choice from Maya's selections was the lemon poppyseed muffin. Maya grabbed a cinnamon bun while Callie declined to take anything. Jason took command at the head of his table with Maya and Callie both setting up on his flanks. Maya's back was to the sliding glass doors where Zoe would always lie in wait, hoping to get a taste of breakfast either during or after the meal. Molly took position beside her, looking hopeful even though Callie had a hard rule of no table food for dogs.

The platter was passed around as each took their desired allocation of breakfast. Conversation held still as first tastes of the eggs and bacon were enjoyed. Jason was focused on his breakfast and muffin when Callie looked at him and Maya for something to talk about. She caught eyes with Maya, smiled, and decided to just start talking.

"So, Maya, your dad tells me that you're studying business?"

Maya looked at her dad with a wonder of what Callie already knew about her.

"This semester," she answered sarcastically while fist bumping her dad. "My mom thinks I should be a teacher. My dad thinks I should study business."

"Both good, I guess," Callie responded.

"What did you study in school?"

Maya asked her question, afraid to call Callie by name. Her dad's friends were always *Mr.* or *Mrs.* or *Ms.* Only Rebecca had succeeded in getting Maya to break the formality, and for her dad to say it was OK to call his peer by her first name.

"I studied graphic design," Callie answered. "I worked in ad agencies in Cleveland and in DC."

"That's cool," Maya said, impressed with Callie's work in advertising.

"Yeah," Callie reflected. "It was."

Maya looked directly at Jason with a big grin.

"Gee, Dad, that fits your plan perfectly," she stated, as if enjoying setting him up for something awkward.

"What's that?" Callie asked, intrigued by Maya's obvious poke at her dad.

Jason sat quietly while Maya's smiling eyes and Callie's desire to learn more gleaned on him.

"It's nothing," he answered, as he looked at his daughter to stifle the humor.

Maya started to laugh at her dad's discomfort, which she felt gave her permission to explain her cryptic comment. Jason sat back for impact while he watched his daughter prepare the explanation he knew was coming.

"My dad said he always said he wanted to marry either an artist or a teacher—"

"Or a nurse," he interjected. "You might as well get it right."

"Yes, that too," Maya confirmed. "Because they could move and work anywhere he had to go."

Callie's eyes rolled from Maya to Jason. She knew the philosophy. She and Jason had talked about when she was in art school. But that context was more about how great it was she was an artist rather than a specific goal to marry one.

"Really?" Callie exclaimed, drawing out the word. "How selfless. How'd that work out for you?"

Callie enjoyed watching Jason squirm to the question. How was he going to defend his plan to marry women in those professions for his own personal career gain all while advocating independence and strength to his own daughter who was studying business?

"Well," he said, sitting forward. "I proved it. I married an MBA and look at what it got me."

Jason's eyes lit up with the confession knowing Maya would find it funny. She had his sense of humor and lived through the decline of his marriage. Callie expected a more defensive and philosophical explanation from "the thinker" and responded with an involuntary belly laugh. As she laughed, her left hand instinctively covered her mouth as Maya looked to her in shared glee. But Maya suddenly stopped laughing as she stared at Callie's hand and the telltale ring on its ring finger.

"So... you're married?" Maya asked, looking at Callie's hand as it fell from her mouth to back under the table.

The room fell silent as Callie looked to Jason for help. Unable to come up with an explanation that could avoid the obvious, he just nodded affirmation to Callie to answer truthfully.

"I am," she said, trying to maintain her dignity that was evaporating.

Maya looked to Jason, waiting for an explanation that would make this be acceptable. He reached for her hand that she immediately pulled away. As her eyes shuffled between them, Maya stood, sliding her chair back to the glass door.

"It's not what you think," Jason said.

His response was to both calm his daughter and to preserve Callie's dignity. Maya responded with a look of disbelief.

"What could I possibly be thinking, Dad?" Maya said, growing emotional. "My divorced dad... from my mom... is having a cozy breakfast after being found snuggling on the bench with a very pretty, MARRIED woman... in fancy pajamas.. at THE BEACH HOUSE. Perfectly normal. Right?"

Callie understood Maya's discomfort and felt a need to step in.

"We didn't—"

Maya did not wait for the explanation to finish. She stormed out through the sliding door after stepping over the sprawled dogs and closing the door in their faces. Jason started to stand, then sat back down to think. Despite having raised four daughters, dealing with emotional outbursts still gave him the need to pause first before engaging in either battle or a solution.

Callie noticed Jason's angst with Maya's response. There was no good way to explain how this all happened. But Callie was a mom who had a daughter and was a daughter herself. Her experience dealing with young women was better than his.

"Let me talk to her," she said, placing her napkin on the table and standing.

They both could see Maya stewing out at the end of the walkway. Callie knew she had limited time to act before Maya would just leave. Jason threw both hands toward his daughter in a gesture giving Callie his permission to try.

"I don't know what good it will do," he said with obvious frustration. "This is where she takes after her mother."

Callie was surprised and disappointed by his comment. But she understood the frustration. Her boys would react just like Chase to situations that would be foreign to her and be best handled by their dad. Although she wasn't Stephanie, and had no idea how Stephanie would handle the situation, she was all Jason had to calm his daughter before she decided to leave in a snit.

"Let me try," she offered. "I have a daughter too."

"Be my guest."

Callie touched Jason's shoulder as she passed by him to imply things would work out. Jason's excitement to have Maya there was gone. What just transpired was beyond belief. As Callie slid the door open, the dogs took their opportunity to head outside with her. Jason watched as Callie made her way down to his daughter.

#

Maya heard both the door and the dogs as they scampered toward her. She then closed the gate to keep Zoe and Molly on the walkway. She looked back to see Callie approaching, rolled her eyes in frustration, and turned away.

As Callie watched Maya stew, she thought to herself that this would be the same scenario with Lizzie regardless if she left Chase or if Chase left her. Lizzie would never understand, and that was a colossal worry. As she approached Jason's youngest daughter, she prepared her opening sentence. This was not a moment she wanted to fumble.

"There's nothing going on between your dad and me," Callie stated with perfect sincerity.

Maya didn't turn. She just looked out over the water as Callie stood next to her.

"I've just figured out who you are," Maya answered, as she turned to look at her. "I can't believe I didn't put it together right away. You're the fiancée. The one that drove all over her parents."

Callie's immediate reaction was to laugh. She held it for as long as she could to not discount the bigger issue. But the humor in it became too much. She started giving in while again covering her mouth with her left hand. Realizing the repeat of the ring reveal that started everything, Callie replaced her left hand with her right. She then looked to Maya who was surprised by her cavalier response and repeat of the reveal that started the turmoil.

"I am her," Callie said, still holding back a lagging smile. "I can't believe he told you that. Although he seems to share it with everyone."

Callie mumbled the finish of her comment as Maya gazed at her in disbelief. This was the woman her dad almost married. The woman who would have had separate children with him, giving them different grandparents and likely a dramatically different life. But even with all the reasons not to like her, Maya concluded quickly that Callie was not a threat to either her or her siblings. Her parents' marriage ended long ago without Callie in the picture. And she was married to some poor sap who apparently did not know this was going on. To Maya, Callie seemed like a good person. She decided to give her the benefit of the doubt.

"You know," Maya stated, "that was the opening for my college essay. It was really about learning from your older sisters. But I opened with that."

Callie was surprised by Maya's shift in direction. Since it was positive, she decided to flow with it.

"Did it work?" she asked, hoping to find common ground instead of working through the misperception that started everything.

"I don't know," Maya answered, appearing to ponder it for the first time. "But it is true about driving over your parents though. I'm not gonna lie about that. I'm not so sure about how well it worked as a college essay."

Callie smiled at the thought of college admission's officers reading her philosophy on birth order and the natural decay of parental influence through it. Maya's discontent for Callie seemed to be easing as they found a sisterhood in being the youngest in a family of girls.

"Feel free to pass that on to your children," Callie said. "I didn't tell mine for obvious reasons."

Maya responded with an obligatory smile, then moved to sit on the bench. Callie followed to join her in the same spot where Maya first discovered her earlier in the morning snuggled next to her dad. As Callie settled in, Maya looked at her as if to say *we're not friends*.

"Do you mind if I sit here?" Callie asked, surprised that the air had chilled.

"It's a free country."

"Look, I know this looks really shady. Me being here—"

"In pajamas," Maya added, in a disapproving tone.

"In pajamas," Callie repeated to confirm her statement.

"Wearing wedding bands."

"Ok," Callie agreed. "Wearing wedding bands."

"Being married."

Maya was working hard to keep a smile at bay. She was through her list of objections and now, just like her dad, was finding sport in making Callie uncomfortable.

"Ok, I think we've covered it," Callie conceded. "But know your dad for who he is. The bottom line is that we have nothing going on. I'm leaving today... going back to DC... back to my life."

"What life is that?"

"A pretty good one," Callie answered, as images of her home and the faces of her kids ran through her head.

"Which is naturally why you are here."

Maya's comment stung Callie back to the present.

"Jeez!" she answered, while throwing her hair back. "You're just like him."

"Apple... tree," Maya answered, savoring the humor through a straight face.

Maya was enjoying running Callie through the pains of the awkward explanation. The apple not falling far from the tree was a reference her dad would often use to explain why kids act like their parents. Callie understood what she meant. Fact of the matter was that once Maya knew who Callie was, everything else made sense, including the acceptance that there was nothing happening between them. She was married. Her dad would honor that. But she was very curious to learn the reason for the weekend and why Callie was there after almost thirty years without them seeing each other. Unless, they had been seeing each other. Maya discarded that thought as soon as she had it. Her dad was always around. Her mom traveled more than he did.

"Yes, well, anyway, I have three kids about your and your sister's ages," Callie continued, trying to answer her question.

"I guess you and my dad have lots in common then."

"We did. We do," Callie answered, pondering her words as she said them.

"And now?" Maya asked, waiting for a declaration about the true status of their relationship.

"Friends, I guess," Callie answered in a deflated voice. "Which is a big step forward from how we left things twenty-seven years ago."

"What's your husband do?"

Maya's curiosity was leading her to inquire further, trying to put pieces into place.

"Politics," Callie answered, almost apologetically. "He fixes and runs big campaigns."

Maya was intrigued by Chase's job, thinking correctly that Callie likely had met a few presidents and been to the White House on different occasions.

"That's cool," was her only thought, which she verbalized without thinking.

"Yup. For him," Callie agreed. "He loves it. Loves it... too much."

The disappointment in Callie's voice was enough for the nineteen-year-old to recognize. Callie did not realize how much their conversation was helping her cope when it was actually Callie's job to bring Maya back to the table.

"Is that why you're here?"

Callie pondered her question for a moment before surrendering.

"I guess."

"Did you find what you were looking for?"

"That's a very mature question for someone so young," Callie replied. "I don't know that answer. Because I don't know what I was looking for."

The conversation flowed so naturally that neither noticed the reversal of roles from consoler to consoled and vice versa. Maya had seen Callie's kind of discontent before as her parents battled through the final years of her high school experience. There was an inevitability that they would not make it. The question was never 'if.' It was just 'when.'

"My dad's been through a lot and he's still not all together," Maya added, further impressing Callie with her mature grasp of what was happening. "They stayed together for me as I finished high school... so I wouldn't crash and burn while applying to college."

"Bad idea?"

"No, but it sucked anyway," Maya acknowledged. "He took a lot of abuse right in front of me. I didn't take them splitting too well. So, it was probably best that I was away at school and didn't have it right in front of me. Both are happier now. So, I'm OK with it."

Callie could tell that Maya still had a lot of things to work out with both her mother and her father. She also knew it was an area that was best left to others to help her with. She started to look for an exit to the conversation as it seemed to have reached a spot where the day could continue with Maya content and Jason happy.

"So, we're good?" Callie asked.

"What choice do I have? Really?" Maya answered. "My mom is just about living with her new boyfriend. It was only a matter of time before my dad found someone."

"I hope you're right," Callie said, pausing to think. "I'm heading back to DC. I've got my family."

"My dad will be upset," Maya answered. "That's for sure. And I AM worried about that."

Callie accepted the compliment with a smile. She reached to touch Maya's arm to give personal assurance that she was not there to inflict any harm on her dad.

"Don't be worried. I'm just an old memory," Callie answered. "But I'm not going to lie either. I kinda hope he feels something."

Maya responded with a reassuring smile that told Callie she 'got it.' Callie moved her hand from Maya's arm to her shoulder to stand up. Maya did not flinch to either touch, which was a good sign. Callie felt confident that she had convinced Maya that her dad's moral compass was still intact.

As their conversation ended in a moment of silent appreciation, they heard a woman's shouting erupt from the beach. They looked to see that people were gathering at the waterline, pointing out into the surf towards a teenage swimmer who was struggling in a riptide that was pulling her out to sea. Their shouted instructions for her to swim with and out of the water's pull were lost to the girl's panic to survive. A few men were wading into the water carrying boogie boards to save her. Their progress was slowed as the waves pounded them back a step for each few steps they were able to take.

Callie was standing at the top of the stairs when she felt a wash of air and shadow streak by. Jason was halfway out on the sand, carrying his flippers in one hand and the life-guard bullet in the other before she figured out what had just happened.

Within seconds, Jason was hurdling the shallow waves, jumping, and nearly stumbling with each step taken. The wave that finally tripped him forward positioned him to dive into the water. After a few seconds under the surf, he emerged swimming freestyle with his flippers on and the bullet trailing behind him on the tether line.

Jason swam past the parents, who were wading out at a pace that made them look like they were standing still. As he passed each one, they surrendered their attempt seeing he was not only going to beat them to the distressed swimmer, but that he had the right lifesaving tools to get her back to shore safely. It was an adrenaline-killing surrender that each adult was happy to make.

Jason adapted his stroke to the Australian crawl to enable him to see his target while continuing at a rapid freestyle pace. He could see the girl was running out of energy, having gone under a few times only to emerge in a burst of coughing to discharge water. Time was growing short as he got near to the victim.

As Jason took his final stroke, his momentum carried him to the girl just as she resurfaced with a flurry of arm action. As he went upright to present the bullet that would give her immediate flotation and calm, she grabbed the top of his head and shoulders to buoy herself higher in the water. Her unexpected weight and push on his body sent him underwater as he was taking a breath. He felt the water rush into his mouth to clog his windpipe as her weight pressed down on him.

As Jason looked up to see the swimmer on top of him, he coughed out into the water that was around him. The girl above him was underwater again, which resulted in her trying harder to climb on him to stay afloat. Her climbing legs kicked his stomach and chest.

Maya and Callie watched the rescue unfold from their perch above the sand on the walkway. Both were frozen in place, fearful of what was happening under the water. Maya grabbed the top of Callie's hand which was gripping the railing. Despite their sure footing, both needed to latch onto something solid.

Jason felt an extreme urgency to breathe as he struggled to fight off the victim who had now attached her legs around him. His thoughts were an unusual appreciation for the girl's incredible strength as she held on for dear life. He felt her grip ease as she became tired from her exertions. As she went to reposition her grip on him, he took his opportunity to separate from her by spinning her body away from him and pushing her away to the surface with his feet.

Jason looked to locate the young girl when he resurfaced for air. He found her within reach, struggling about five feet away. He immediately shoved the bullet at her with instructions to grab it. As she grabbed the white flotation device, she gained immediate lift and calm. Her peace gave Jason the opportunity to regain his composure. After waiting a moment to calm himself and her, Jason began to swim them parallel to the shoreline to release from the grab of the rip current.

Maya and Callie exhaled in relief when they saw Jason emerge from under the water safely with the girl under control. Both knew he would not have given up on her, even to his own demise.

As Jason and the girl gained footing in the surf, the boogie board parents surrounded them to assist taking the girl to shore. Rebecca, who had been watching from the beach, met the girl at the waterline to help her onto sandy beach to provide immediate medical care. Jason lumbered out slowly behind the crowd, exhausted from the effort.

"What the heck just happened?" Callie asked.

"My dad just saved that girl."

"And just about got killed in the process."

Callie's comment exhibited more anger for the dangerous risk than pride in the end result. Jason's heroics could have cost him his life. From her observation there were younger and fitter adults on the shoreline watching the girl struggle. It did not seem necessary that he, at fifty-five, and just having been reintroduced to her, should have to take such a deadly risk.

The irony that what just happened almost played out Callie's initial wishes to Sandy in their phone conversation for *Jason to drown in the rip currents* did not occur to Callie until long after the weekend was over. Now that normalcy was returning and their heart rates had calmed, Callie and Maya descended the stairs to the sand to meet their returning hero.

Jason's trek back to the cottage was slow. He was both exhausted from the effort and slowed by the gratitude of the girl's family. When Callie and Maya reached him, he had separated from all of the attention and was on his way back to them.

Both women had the same desire to hug their hero. Callie saw Maya in her peripheral vision move toward her dad and stopped to let his daughter be the one to express her thankfulness for what he had done, and that he was still with them.

Maya's hug was long and deep as a daughter's appreciation for her dad should be. Jason dropped his flippers and bullet to return her embrace as if Maya had been the rescuer. Callie picked up Jason's flippers as he let go of his daughter. He then reached out his arm to give her a one-armed hug.

"That was kinda insane," Callie stated, as Jason released his hold on her.

"They just didn't have the right gear," he responded nonchalantly to avoid discussion on a possible grim outcome that did not happen.

"Is she OK?" Maya asked.

"Yeah," Jason answered. "Rebecca's watching her for shock. She's really scared. But she'll be fine."

"Are you OK?" Callie asked.

Her voice was full of concern that added fresh wind to Jason's sail. He smiled in appreciation. Two days earlier, he would have bet the cottage Callie would have preferred he had sunk while saving the girl in the rescue.

"What? Me?" he answered. "Yeah. I'm OK."

Jason's cavalier reply was followed by a quick towel-off of his hair and face. As he pulled himself back together, he noted that both women were staring at him in disbelief.

"What?" he asked, clueless to their thoughts because he was fine.

"Dad, that was pretty dicey," Maya answered in a seriousness that rarely showed. "We weren't so sure you were coming back up."

Callie grabbed Jason's hand while giving him a look that told him that the rest of the world had just stopped for her. He treasured her look of concern and gratification that he was safe.

"Dad!" Maya interjected, breaking the moment.

"Ehh, just another day at the beach," Jason replied, then smiled with his next thought. "But that certainly would've made it awkward for you two."

Callie released Jason's hand with a rumbled laugh of disbelief to the comment.

"Oh my God. You didn't just make a joke about that."

## 15

With the bacon and eggs breakfast now cold and ruined, the only edibles left were in the box of pastries Maya brought earlier. Jason ordered the two women out of his kitchen so he could clean up the mess and give him something ordinary to think about as he calmed down from the rescue. Maya took the opportunity to gather her stuff from her car to settle in for the day. Whether or not she was staying overnight remained to be seen. Callie went to check her phone for the messages she knew were waiting and dreaded.

As her screen illuminated, a missed call from Lizzie appeared in her phone's notifications. Callie's anxiety returned as she recalled her promise to call Lizzie the previous day that went unfulfilled. She sat on her bed and pushed 'call back.'

"Lizzie? Hey, it's Mom," she said before Lizzie could finish hello. "Sorry, honey, about not getting back to you."

The line held silent for a moment, which concerned her.

"Where are you?" Lizzie asked, in an annoyed voice. "Dad says you're at the beach. He's asking me who we know at the Outer Banks."

Callie's stomach dropped as Lizzie probed her location. How would Chase know she was at the Outer Banks? Why would he call Lizzie with questions? It then occurred to her that she left Carolyn the cryptic note about heading to the beach. That realization offered short-lived relief as anxiety of not calling her mother yesterday started to build within her.

"Honey, I'm visiting an old Cleveland friend," Callie replied, keeping it simple and true as Chase would tell his clients when circumventing a negative. "Your dad is playing golf with his friends. I was going to be alone. So, I'm visiting with an old friend."

"That sounds like fun," Lizzie answered in an uplifted tone. "Ya know. I like the beach too. Is the weather nice? Isn't it raining?"

Callie felt relief to be off the 'who' and onto the 'what' of her trip. She wanted to keep pushing the focus away from who the Cleveland 'friend' was so that her untruths could be held to exclusion instead of made into lies.

"I know you like the beach," Callie answered, visualizing Lizzie's response to the situation if she knew the truth. "I honestly don't think you'd have fun here. No rain either. It's fine. Maybe next time!"

Callie winced at the words as they came out. The thought of Lizzie's complete rejection of anything outside of Callie being married to Chase played over and over in her mind as Lizzie spoke words Callie did not hear.

"Callie?" Jason called from the hallway, unaware she was on the phone.

He knocked then cracked open the door to find Callie with a panicked expression. Her hand was up to direct him to not talk. As his eyes met hers, Callie's eyes closed to concentrate on a remedy to get out of the conversation in a way that would not raise suspicion. He rolled back into the hallway to give her call some privacy.

"Who's that?" Lizzie asked, recognizing the male voice tone.

"That's," Callie said, then paused to think. "That's my friend… Stephanie's husband."

She then called out to answer Jason's call.

"I'm on the phone. I'll be out in a minute."

Jason understood the unraveling situation. Frozen in place, he looked back down the hallway for Maya to see if a female voice could be added into the background mix of people. She was outside with the dogs.

"Does Dad know Stephanie? I have to call him back."

"I don't think so, sweetie," Callie answered, paining through her first lies to her daughter. "She wasn't at our wedding, and I haven't seen her since I moved to DC."

"How'd you find her this weekend?" Lizzie responded.

"Facebook," Callie answered quickly as if nothing. "Look, sweetie, I have to go. I PROMISE I'll call you tomorrow."

"Ok, Mom," Lizzie answered in a surprisingly soft tone of understanding. "I'm glad you found something fun to do. Love you."

Callie both winced and smiled as she listened to her daughter's parting words of affection. The last call did not end as well, which led Callie to believe Lizzie was in a good place.

"Love you too, sweetie. Bye."

Jason was surprised to see Callie wearing a smile when he looked in to check on her. He only heard parts of her side of the conversation that seemed quite precarious. As she placed the phone down on her bedspread, Callie exhaled, showing some confidence that, at least for now, her secret was secure.

"Everything OK?"

"I think so. But I'm not sure."

# # #

The view from the villa's terrace included the eighth green and ninth tee of the golf course. Chase sat in the warmth of the autumn sun to recover from his first of two rounds of golf scheduled for the day. As with the rest of his family, his habits led him to turn his attention to his phone and its content of texts, emails, and other critical superfluous items that would appear on a Sunday morning.

As his screen lit, he noted just missing a text from Lizzie. Before teeing off for the early round, he had texted her to find out who they knew that vacationed on the Outer Banks and would invite her mother for a last-minute getaway weekend. Lizzie's first response was a 'IDK'. He challenged her to find out through direct contact with her mom.

Just spoke to mom. At beach with Stephanie from cleve. Said home tomorrow.

Stephanie from Cleveland was a name Chase could not place. Of all Callie's friends he had met over the years from Cleveland, college, and DC, he could not recall meeting a 'Stephanie'. He picked up his phone to find out who Stephanie was to Callie.

"Hello?" Carolyn answered on her cordless phone from the garden.

"Hi Carolyn, it's Chase. Is Callie there?"

Carolyn was as much puzzled by Chase's inquiry as she was by Callie's unannounced arrival late Friday, followed by her early morning departure on Saturday. Carolyn's public rule was always to be honest and to stay out of her children's spousal squabbles. But her number one rule was to protect her daughters from everything she could so that, no matter the trouble, they would have opportunity to recover and to fix whatever needed fixing.

"No, Callie is not here. She arrived Friday night and was gone Saturday before I got up. I was surprised. Left me a note about seeing a friend at the beach."

Despite it being the absolute truth, the vagueness of Carolyn's response raised Chase's suspicions.

"Oh," he said. "I think that's Stephanie from Cleveland."

Chase put Stephanie's name out to see how Carolyn would react and maybe fill in a backstory that made sense for Callie's immediate and suspicious run to the beach. Her response took a moment to compile.

"Stephanie?" Carolyn answered, not recognizing the name. "Chase, I don't know. She didn't say."

Carolyn succeeded in her goal to stay within the confines of both rules.

"Ok," he replied. "I'll try her cell again."

Carolyn was relieved to have him end his hunt for Callie through her. But the intrigue of where Callie had run to just got enhanced by the unfamiliar name she had never known as one of Callie's friends from Cleveland. The unfolding mystery made her start to think that something was not right.

"That'd be best, Chase," Carolyn agreed. "Bye."

Carolyn hung up then sat on a cast-iron bench that she and her husband bought in a Colonial Williamsburg antiques store the first month they lived in Virginia. Her hand ran across the carved surface as she reached out to Callie's dad for guidance.

"Oh Callie," she mumbled to herself. "What on earth are you up to?"

#

Chase thought back through his conversation with Carolyn. Although he knew her to be the frankest person he had ever met when sharing what she thought and knew, he also knew her commitment to her daughters was over anything and everything else. Something was clearly 'off' about Callie's whereabouts. She was off his radar and that was beginning to concern him. He had to go find her.

As he exited his room with his weekend bag, Chase's golf partner, Sabby, had just finished top dressing a three-inch-thick turkey sandwich with an array of condiments that would offend most palates. Sabby first noticed Chase's accelerated pace with the expectation that he would make the turn into the bathroom for an urgent pitstop. But, when Chase passed the couch to expose his weekend bag could, Sabby knew he was leaving. His response to that revelation was to immediately throw down his sandwich and vector a course to cut his golf partner off before he reached the door.

"Bud, we have a tee time in fifty minutes," Sabby stated while placing himself between Chase and the door.

"Sorry, man. I've got to go," Chase responded, as he successfully jostled around him to get outside. "I'll call you."

Chase grabbed his clubs off the golf cart parked near the front door and threw them into the back of his Maserati. He then tossed his weekend bag onto the front passenger seat. Sabby watched while trying to figure out something to convince him to stay. He knew from his actions that Chase was upset. Throwing things was not out of the ordinary when Chase was mad, particularly on the golf course. But throwing his precious golf clubs into the back of his precious car painted an entirely different picture. He had to do something.

Sabby moved quickly to place the golf cart behind the Maserati to pin Chase in. He then approached and tapped on his driver's window to check on his friend. After taking a moment, Chase rolled the window down while the motor continued to hum.

"What's wrong, Bubba?" Sabby asked.

"Nothing," Chase answered, as he avoided eye contact with his best friend. "Gotta go."

"Dude, it's Sunday, and tomorrow's a freaking holiday. What's the rush?"

Chase continued his stare forward, contemplating all the details and holes in what he knew about Callie's weekend.

"Callie was really pissed that I came here after being away for work."

Chase admitted this only to convince his best friend to MOVE THE FUCKING GOLF CART! But Sabby stayed composed as he tried to calm and convince his golf partner to stay.

"I think all the wives were pissed," he replied, trying to add empathy to his tone. "They should've been included."

Sabby's comment was such a lie that Chase cracked a smile. Both men would agree that women would have ruined the sanctity of their boys' weekend. Although he pressed to hold from laughing, Chase finally gave in to the pressure and released a chuckle. As he looked at his friend in appreciation for what he just said, a reality washed over him to change his smile to a serious look of concern.

"This is different, Bud. Callie's gone dark on the phone. Now she's at the beach with an old friend I don't know... I don't know what the fuck is going on."

Sabby saw real concern in his friend's face. He knew he had to be supportive and provide a light of reason Chase would find comforting.

"So naturally you're just going to rush there?" he answered. "Dude, bad idea. I think you should think about that again. She just made this all golden for you to stay here."

Sabby's counsel was contrary to what Chase was thinking. Chase looked at his friend who, over the years, had put him into and pulled him out of a lot of dicey situations. Sabby's logic was simple, as it always was, to grasp the moment in a way that solved the problem.

"You just got your gold pass to stay," he continued without hesitation and thought. "Just keep pinging her with texts that you're sorry. It'll blow over like it always does."

Chase considered his friend's wisdom. It made sense up until the point he remembered that his best friend in the world was not married, and that all of his relationships failed miserably, usually because of his callous disregard for anyone's feelings but his own. But then again, he could be also right.

"I guess," Chase finally agreed. "You're sure about all that?"

Sensing a victory to keep his friend on the golf course for the second round of the day versus on the road, Sabby nodded.

"As sure as I'm standing here," he answered, now smiling out of confidence that they were back in the match that was about to tee off.

Chase pulled the Maserati back up into its spot, turned off its engine, and got out. As he pulled his clubs out of the car to return them to their spot on the cart, he turned to his friend of thirty years.

"You better be fucking right."

"Dude," was all Sabby could say while holding his hands out and spinning to reorient himself back toward the turkey sandwich he had left on the counter.

## 16

Callie was still reeling from her conversation with Lizzie that included a number of first-time lies. She recalled talks that Carolyn had with her that she, in turn, had with Lizzie and her brothers about honesty. Lies, her mother would say, only build on themselves to reach a breaking point. For a moment, Callie felt a sense of comfort in carrying on that wisdom with her children. Her smile of satisfaction, however, evaporated when her phone started to vibrate and chime the church bell ringtone she had set exclusively to her mom.

Callie took her time to reach for the phone, as if counting through the vibrations to answer too late. The conversation she expected was one she did not want to have, let alone have and be able to keep her spirits up for the rest of the day. She let the call go to voicemail.

"Ready?" Jason asked, poking his head into Callie's room.

He had timed his inquiry to the non-answering of the phone. The church bells gave him a good idea of who the caller was. Had Callie answered, he would have stepped away until the call was over. Or so he was telling himself. Callie looked sad at first glance, then put on a happy face to answer.

"Yeah," she answered, while stumbling through thought. "YES. Let's go out to the beach."

Callie then stood to organize the things she had collected. She put her phone into her pocket, thinking she could check messages and texts as time would permit. Jason was happy to see her transition to a happier self as she walked by him and started down the hallway. After a few steps she stopped to think.

"Maya took chairs down," he said, as he walked by her.

"Ya know what? I'll be a few minutes. I'll meet you there."

Callie then gave him a reassuring touch on his arm.

# # #

Maya had the chairs set in a row near the hightide's water mark in the sand. The surf was still choppy and heavy despite the sunshine that had chased the storms away. Maya intentionally sat on an end chair, anxious to see if Jason would either sit next to her as a buffer or put Callie in the hot seat between them. With ear-pods in, she did not hear him walk up from behind, and was startled when he plopped down into the chair next to her.

Maya immediately pulled her pods from her ears expecting an opening remark from her dad. He had a habit of speaking first regarding anything that was happening. Listening to his initial statement often provided a 'temperature' on his disposition. It was a lesson Maya learned from her older sisters which was included as part of her college essay. This time, however, Jason just looked off into the distance, waiting for Maya to surrender her unsolicited opinion of the situation and, more so, of Callie.

"She's nice," Maya finally stated, knowing and enjoying the fact that she knew he wanted to hear her opinions.

"She is nice."

"And married," Maya added deliberately. "Seriously, Dad! Married? What's going on? Am I going to hear about my dad being murdered by some jealous husband?"

Jason smirked at the comment since it was almost the same question he had asked Callie.

"I hope not."

Jason knew his answer would needle his daughter for not being more honest with either himself or the situation.

"I'm not finding this funny."

"I honestly don't know much," Jason confessed to ease her concern. "She appeared yesterday. I don't know if she's running... or just blowing off steam."

"How'd she find you? You two just didn't run into each other."

Maya had started putting the pieces together concerning their situations and geography. Their weekend was not accidental. She knew there were more pieces than she knew, and that her dad was not sharing. She also wondered if either her dad or Callie had a bigger picture vision that they were keeping from the other.

"How does anyone find anyone these days?" Jason answered to tell his daughter to think of the obvious.

Maya smiled when she linked the known pieces together.

"I saw your post," she replied. "Are you going to be OK when she leaves?"

"Sure," he answered. "Why wouldn't I be?"

"Because she's your one."

Maya's reply was without hesitation. Her look was sincere and serious. It was not the typical relationship joking they had when trying to make specific points about an awkward father/daughter topic. Jason studied her face and eyes in amazement wondering *when did this little girl grow up?*

"Why do you say that?"

"Oh, come on," Maya replied in disbelief. "She's the only old girlfriend you talked about every chance you got. And Mom always cringed hearing her name, which YOU THOUGHT WAS FUNNY. And... she's beautiful."

The last comment struck Jason the hardest. She was still beautiful. She was beautiful at eighteen, twenty-three, and now at fifty. It started at skin level and radiated through every cell of her being. She was the fireball youngest daughter who wanted to earn everything herself, and gave everything she had at the expense of herself. Jason inhaled to counter the pressure of the tears of pride and happiness that were building inside him.

"She is beautiful," he finally confessed, "but it doesn't matter because she's married... and that ends it there."

It was rare for Jason to show emotion in front of Maya. He always maintained the tough dad composure that she loved about him. But that love was also built on the times she would sometimes hear him off in the darkness, crying to release the stresses in his life and sadness of his losses. Her dad became human to her then as she witnessed the unraveling of her parents' marriage and their other stresses over the past ten years. She never shared with him what she knew. She knew his strength was the bedrock of their relationship.

"Would you marry her if she divorced her husband?"

"No," Jason answered abruptly.

"Really?" she asked, surprised by how matter of fact his answer was.

"No," he repeated, just as fast as the first time. "It's not possible. So why speculate?"

"Come on, play along. Live with her?"

"What?" he asked.

"Date her?"

"What are you asking me?" he replied, looking to stop her inquisition.

"I'm just wondering. Your aura is much brighter, like, happier," Maya answered. "You look a lot happier."

Jason surveyed his daughter's smiling face with a questioning look. She was right. He was riding an emotional high with Callie's visit. But the overcast of her inevitable departure and return to her husband and family made fantasizing about anything more, particularly with his daughter there, a growing stress.

"Where did that come from?" he asked.

His question came with a slight laugh of embarrassment. His change of attitude made Maya wonder if her dad was now using her questions to seek more insight from her on his relationship with Callie. His look was optimistic as he waited for her to say something either 'insightfully helpful' he could use, or 'catastrophically wrong' that he could shoot holes into.

"I'm just sayin'," she answered cautiously, "that you two look like you belong together... And that's your kid saying that."

The end qualifier amused Jason. Just as he saw his youngest prodigy as an adult full of worldly wisdom, she knocked his perspective of her back to her youthful innocence to prove how obvious the pull between him and Callie was to those on the outside looking in. And, as all of her observations settled into his head, he still knew the most critical part of the equation that Maya did not know. Callie was an extraordinarily loyal person. Her kids, her promises, and her life commitments would always come before her happiness.

"We're both working off twenty-five... twenty-seven-year-old feelings and images of each other from a relationship that did NOT end well," he commented, intentionally leaving out lots of the other details. "And, she's married now with a family. I don't know why she's here. But you just don't ditch all of that for something that didn't work out decades ago, particularly after just a two-day beach weekend."

Maya watched her dad finish what he had to say, not sure if she felt he believed it all himself.

"Who cares where, when, or how it starts just so long as the ending's right?" she replied, growing frustrated with his defeatist attitude.

Maya's tone was defiant. She had had many conversations with both Jason and others about her own 'you only live once' mantra. A mantra centered on many of their soccer trip windshield conversations regarding life decisions for Maya as she progressed through sport, school, and life. And, although it should never be used as an excuse to crush or hurt anyone, 'you only live once' should also never be bypassed to surrender life's opportunities and enjoyment. There had to be a balance.

"That's just it," Jason replied, obviously frustrated. "The RIGHT ending won't be this."

As he finished his thought, he kicked the sand under his feet. He then looked away, embarrassed to have let go in front of his daughter.

"You don't know that!" Maya exclaimed, growing more frustrated and animated with her dad. "Finding you may have been brewing in her longer than just two days ago. Maybe she just had no way to connect with you?"

Jason smiled then exhaled in amusement at the absurdity of Maya's statement.

"There are ways, easy ways, to find people and to connect. Very private ways too."

Jason hoped his revelation would cap the conversation for good.

"Maybe she was afraid YOU'D reject HER," Maya replied softly.

Jason pondered Maya's insight for a moment. It would be against Callie's nature to reach out. His last communication with her about her dad was sterile. It was written in a manner to maintain the respect for their boundaries. And it got no response. His treatment of her through the breakup of their engagement was cold and arguably mean. She had no reason to believe he was not gone for good, which led him to wonder why she was suddenly there.

"Maybe you should study law," he declared to her surprise while invoking a new panic of parental life and study intrusion in Maya.

## 17

Callie relished the wash of the warm, humid breeze across her face as she stepped through the sliding glass door and away from the air conditioning. As she walked out across the wood planking, she could see Jason and Maya deep in conversation while seated on their chairs by the water's edge. It reminded her of similar times she had with each of her children through their many vacations on Nantucket Island. Times that were changing into new adult experiences that would soon add grandchildren. Callie stopped walking as that thought deflated her happiness.

As she stood and watched her two, waiting beach-mates banter back and forth, her phone vibrated with the familiar ringtone that was Chase. She let the phone cycle a few times through its vibrations before answering.

"Hey, honey," Chase opened, not waiting to hear Callie's voice.

"What do you want, Chase?" she replied in a cold monotone.

"Just to hear your voice."

"And now you have. Goodbye."

Callie began to pull her phone away from her ear to hang up when she heard Chase respond quickly with 'Lizzie.'

"LIZZIE says you're at the beach with Stephanie," he said in a rushed tone. "I don't remember Stephanie."

"Stephanie Cartwright," Callie blurted without thinking.

The natural put together of the two names that went together at one time happened unconsciously before she could think and act to stop it. Chase knew about Jason and hoped his last name was not something he would pull from his active memory. She had to push on with more information to overwhelm and confuse his recollections away from that recall. It was a tactic Chase said he used often when he explained many funny campaign situations solved by throwing overwhelming pile of worthless information at probing reporters.

"She's..." Callie stumbled as her thoughts gelled. "She's a school friend from home. You don't know her. She didn't come to our wedding because she lived out of town. I found her on Facebook Friday after you left and connected. She invited me down since I was so close... and alone."

Callie added guilt to the load of confusion she was trying to build in Chase's head as he processed her explanation.

"THAT'S GREAT!" he replied, obviously puzzled. "But I thought I met all your friends from home. Well, I'm glad you found something fun to do besides seeing your mom."

"If you say so," Callie responded quickly, continuing to pressure the guilt nerve. "Look, I'm expected on the beach. I've got to go."

"Wait! Don't you want to talk about this?" Chase asked, desperate to hold on to their conversation.

"Now?" Callie replied with a pause. "No, Chase, I don't. I was in a good place until you called. Please just leave me alone. No more calls. No more texts. Give me some space. Go play some FUCKING GOLF!"

Callie pushed 'end' just as she completed her final dig. It was encouraging to her that he was feeling guilt. Or, at least, that he was making an effort to make her think he felt guilty. Both were wins. But those feelings were also strong counter-emotions to what she was living through currently with Jason. She felt a bind of no escape start to tighten around her as she moved her eyes from her phone back out to the father-daughter duo that was waiting for her.

#

As Callie descended the stairs and stepped off to feel the grains of the sand between her toes, Jason stood to respond to Zoe and Molly who had just dropped a tennis ball at his feet. Molly had no retrieving instinct. But she was content to run with Zoe to stop short of the rolling water as Zoe would fetch and return Jason's tosses. Zoe's game was to drop the ball short of Jason making him move further down the beach with each throw.

Jason was walking along the waterline as the water washed up and over his feet. His focus was on Zoe jumping through the waves as Molly stayed more with him than as Zoe's wingman. Callie walked up from behind, lifted his arm, and nested in beside him.

"I think my cover is falling apart," she admitted in a quiet voice.

"Cover?" he qualified. "Are you telling me you're not who you say you are?"

Jason smiled while enjoying the absurdity of his question. But his disposition quickly changed to concern when Callie did not return even a fake smile. She was struggling.

"I don't know if that's the right word," she answered. "I think my family is on to where I am, and who I'm with."

Jason thought through the possibilities and decided the likelihood of her being discovered was nearly impossible unless she told someone.

"You're being paranoid," he replied, to reassure her that everything was fine.

"I don't think so. My phone's been lighting up a lot today. Lizzie was quizzing me. They know I'm at the beach because I left my mom a note that said I was visiting a friend. So, I had to lie to her. I told her I was with Stephanie."

Jason looked away so she would not see him struggle to not burst into laughter. He then bent over to pick up a broken shell to buy more time. As he handed his find to Callie, she threw it back into the surf without a look. No appreciation for the effort, and no snide remark about the crappy shell, told him she was in a panic.

"Stephanie? Seriously? You couldn't come up with a different name?"

The question was half serious and half jab to lighten the moment. The only person who could connect a Stephanie to him was Carolyn. And that from a brief encounter twenty-five years ago and likely forgotten.

"I know," Callie admitted. "I panicked. I told her that she's an old friend her dad doesn't know."

"Well, that's not a complete lie."

Jason's attempt to make it a joke resulted in a stern look of disapproval.

"Your mother might remember," he then pondered out loud. "Would your mother remember Stephanie?"

"I don't think so," she answered. "Fuck."

"What?"

"My mother called this morning too."

"And?"

"I didn't take it," she confessed. "I let it roll to voicemail."

"Did she leave a message?"

Zoe had been patiently moving the ball closer to Jason and Callie as they talked. The ball washed over Jason's foot, which he lifted to grab the ball as it returned to him in the wash of the water. As he picked up the ball, they turned to head back towards the chairs.

"I didn't check for her message," Callie answered about the voicemail. "Maybe I should."

"You think!?"

 As Callie pondered his question, Jason bent down again to pick up an intact snail-shaped shell from the surf. The conversation with her mother would be difficult and likely have additional lies she knew *would build upon themselves to break.* Callie accepted and started to study the shell Jason handed to her.

"I don't know if I should," she answered. "I'm going to get caught, which I deserve. Maybe."

Rebecca appeared in their vision as Callie finished her declaration. Both their faces morphed from concern to joy to greet her as they knew she had news on Jason's earlier rescue.

"Hey y'all," Rebecca called out, as she finished her last few steps towards them.

"How's that little girl?" Callie asked as a mother who had, many times, feared the same for her children.

"Very frightened," Rebecca answered. "But she's OK thanks to Baywatch here."

Rebecca could not hold back a big smile with the jab she knew would embarrass Jason in front of his love interest. She also knew that everyone loves a hero. So, her endorsement of his actions could not hurt his opportunities with Callie.

"They never would've reached her," Jason replied, to downplay the rescue.

"Oh Jason, I'm just messing with you," Rebecca joked back. "You saved the day. Seriously, you did."

Rebecca touched his arm in sincere appreciation for his effort and for him. Embarrassed, he did not respond to the recognition. Callie looked to Rebecca in shared amusement in the rare awkwardness shown by their hero.

"So, Callie," Rebecca asked. "Will you be here for cocktails? We're staying until tomorrow. My kids have Columbus Day off. So, we'll be here tonight."

Rebecca showed a giddy enthusiasm that there was going to be one more day at the beach. Fall on the North Carolina shore was typically filled with days of glorious sunshine and warmth when the rest of the mid-Atlantic on northward was starting to deal with the rain and cold of fall. The regular interferences of school and child activities made fall weekends less frequent as kids got older. Jason recalled great memories of fall soccer with his kids. He knew he would have chosen athletics over the ocean if he would have had the choice back then.

"I don't think I'm staying," Callie replied. "I think I'll probably head home today."

"That's too bad," Rebecca answered, looking back and forth between the two. "It's such a nice day. One of the final few that shouldn't be spent in the car."

Callie appreciated the sincerity of Rebecca's comment as genuine to keep her around for the party.

"That's true... I'll try," she replied, as she felt her very loose plan to leave nudge back towards staying another night.

Rebecca smiled encouragement. "Well, good, nice to see you again Callie. See YOU later, Jason."

Rebecca backed away then turned to leave as Callie dropped the shell Jason had handed her.

"You should stay," he said, while reaching down to pick up what she just discarded. "And you should keep shells people give you. It's the polite thing to do... and it's good luck."

Callie responded with a look of worry Jason hoped would not be the demise of the rest of the weekend.

"That's just it. I think I'm pushing my luck," she confessed, looking for support to convince her otherwise.

"You should stay," he advocated. "And you should call your mother back. You can say 'hi' from me."

Jason nudged her with the suggestion as they started to walk back toward the chairs near the cottage. Zoe watched in desperation, still waiting for the ball to fly as all of Jason's attention had shifted away from her to Callie. As the ball washed back and forth in the surf, Molly took advantage of Zoe's distraction to grab it and run towards her mom whose attention was also now on someone new.

As they approached the chairs Maya had set out earlier, Jason took a moment to survey a cluster of shells on the beach. He dug into the sand to pull an unusually large and complete clam-shaped shell full of rings of bright color from under a pile of broken fragments. As fast as he handed the wiped-off perfect specimen to her, Callie threw it into the ocean as she continued to ponder her fate.

"You've got to take shells home," he declared to call her back into present time. "You've told everyone you're at the beach."

# # #

As Jason and Callie returned to their chairs in the sand, Maya walked toward them from the house stairs. She had changed back into shorts and a long sleeve Wolfpack t-shirt.

"Hey, I'm going to head back to school if that's OK."

"You just got here," Jason replied, surprised by his daughter who loved the ocean.

"I know," she answered. "But there's stuff going on. And I THINK I have classes tomorrow."

Callie smiled at the obvious lie, knowing Maya was making herself scarce.

"Think?" Jason asked. "You don't know?"

Maya looked back and forth between them while nodding her head *yes*. The smile on her face showed Callie that she was accepting her being there which made her happy and nervous at the same time. The visit was obviously building expectations that were not going to happen.

"Dad. Clue in. You two have a lot to talk about. I'll just be in the way."

Jason was embarrassed that he was the only one of the three who did not see Maya's true purpose for leaving so soon. He looked at Callie for a sign of hope. He then looked back at Maya to grant his unneeded permission for her to go.

"Stay," Callie announced, uncomfortable with the growing situation. "We can make it all work. I don't think I'm staying, anyway."

Surprised and panicked by Callie's declaration, Jason quickly turned to look at her.

"See that, Dad!?" Maya proclaimed. "That's what I'm talking about. You two need to talk while you can."

Jason's reaction was Maya's reassurance that her decision to go was the right thing to do. She looked sadly out to the water to say goodbye to such a fantastic afternoon. But she also knew she would be back and wanted those visits to be with her dad in a very happy place.

Callie watched Jason as he considered Maya's comments without responding, completely unaware of the silence that surrounded him. Maya, taking her moment to exit, walked to her dad and hugged him.

"OK, sweetie," he said softly, accepting her kindness.

Maya released Jason and turned to hug Callie goodbye. Callie accepted Maya's hug awkwardly while looking at Jason. His eyes showed tears as Callie's arms closed around his daughter.

"It's kinda cool to put the person with the legend," Maya said as they separated.

"I hope I get to see you again," Callie replied, appreciative of the generosity Maya had extended to her.

"Me too," Maya answered, returning to the age and attitude Callie would have expected.

After a few glances back and forth between the three, Maya touched Jason's shoulder as she turned to walk away.

"Go Cavs," she said to her dad, who shared her love of the Cleveland Cavaliers.

"Go Cavs," he laughed, while wiping a tear from his eyes.

Callie marveled at the relationship and care Jason extended toward Maya during her stay. It was obvious to her that he had been a good father to his children. It was his nature, which she would have loved to have both witnessed and shared.

"What a wonderful young woman," she said as she watched Maya walk away. "And, oh my God, you're such a softie."

Jason and Callie watched Maya stop to chat with Rebecca. They both looked back and waved. Rebecca then hugged Maya, who shared a few departing words before she walked up and over the stairs back to the cottage. Zoe and Molly followed her up and onto the walkway, then returned.

"You know what?" Jason said, still enjoying his moment of pride. "I'm going to run up to the house to use the bathroom and to give Maya some cash for gas, for the doughnuts, ya know... I'll be back. Want anything to drink?"

"Surprise me," Callie answered as she settled into one of the beach chairs. She knew Maya had to have a credit card with Jason's name on it. So, giving cash was just another show of affection a dad could give his daughter before returning to school. Or, in her case, a mom showing the same love for her children as they left on their adventures.

Jason jogged to the stairs and made his way up and out of sight over the dune. Callie felt relief to be by herself. She pulled out her phone to check messages.

## 18

The cordless phone lit and rang as it sat on the granite countertop of the kitchen island. Carolyn had just sat on a nearby stool to enjoy her lunch and iced tea after a morning of gardening. The kitchen television was on with the cooking show that she watched daily to find new recipes to adapt to her palate and diet. A small box appeared in the corner of her television screen with Callie's name and phone number 'calling.' Carolyn muted her show to answer.

"Hi, Mom," Callie said without waiting for her mom to say anything.

For the first time, Callie was felt guilt about having visited her mother unannounced only to disappear without warning. She was now ready to deal with the fallout that was to come.

"Callie," Carolyn said, relieved to hear her voice. "I've been worried about you. Chase called early this morning looking for you. I tried calling you and got your voicemail."

Callie was surprised, relieved, and somewhat disheartened that her mother's reaction was one of concern than of disappointment. Typically, Carolyn would chastise first, then, if needed, follow with compassion to ease the situation. This was the second time Callie could remember Carolyn leading with compassion when things went awry. The first time was just after the engagement split with Jason.

"I'm fine, Mom. I'm at the beach," Callie answered. "What did you tell him?"

"What I knew," Carolyn answered. "You went to the shore to visit a friend."

Callie was relieved to hear that her mom did not speculate with Chase on her whereabouts.

"You KNOW where I am, don't you?" she asked, probing to see if her mother could have accidently slipped any speculation into her conversation with Chase.

"Something tells me I don't want to know," Carolyn answered. "I do want to know that you are OK, and that you're not doing anything you'll regret."

"It's not like that."

Carolyn's chest tightened with thoughts she would never have pondered for Callie.

"It may not be," she admonished. "But things aren't always seen for what they are."

"I'm sorry, Mom," Callie answered, regretting the disappointment she just caused. "I just called to check in and to let you know that I am fine. I'll drive through tomorrow on my way back to DC."

"Well, that's good to hear."

Callie was puzzled by her mother's reply.

"I wouldn't just drive by without stopping."

"That's not what I meant. I'm glad you're going back home."

The depth of her mother's concern was exposed in that single statement. Callie closed her eyes as she pondered the thoughts and disappointment her mother had in her youngest daughter. The sisters' pact to keep Mom clear of all worry and anxiety had just been obliterated by Callie's reckless decision to not only sneak down to see Jason, but to use her mother's house as a pitstop on the way. In hindsight, just pretending to have stayed in Great Falls would have been a smarter play. Great Falls was home. And until that moment, not going back home was never a thought.

"Where else am I expected to be?" Callie replied to put her mom's mind at ease.

But the tradition of honesty between them, along with the little girl still inside her still wanting to prove her independence, pushed past her willpower to keep her secret to herself. Her next confession pulverized the sisters' pact. It also released an unbearable weight of guilt off her shoulders. Her mother had to know.

"By the way," Callie continued, hesitating to finish her confession. "Jason says 'hello.'"

Carolyn made no immediate response to the news, which concerned Callie. Never in the past, when she had done something so wrong, had her mother not had an immediate response of piercing disappointment. That was her way to stop the bleeding in order to start work on the healing. But this time, there was nothing. Callie may have gone too far.

"Jason? Jason Cartwright!?" finally emerged through the line in eerily calm, quiet tone of disbelief. "Don't tell me you're with Jason now?"

Callie paused to deal with the guilt that washed back across the relief she had briefly enjoyed.

"It's not what you think," she answered.

"Oh, Callie," Carolyn replied. "What are you doing?"

The worry in her mother's voice was deep, adding to the guilt that was already building within her. In her mind, Callie knew the weekend had an overtone of innocence and that Jason was being a complete gentleman despite opportunities created by her to hint there could be more. Buy she was also insulted that her own mother would think the worst without first trusting her judgement. But, as Callie thought through their last conversation that was loaded with details of disappointment about her marriage, it became clear that her mother had a compelling reason to fear the worst for the visit.

"We're just talking," Callie answered, failing to realize that she was not painting a clear picture of what they were talking about.

"You have a family, and a husband," Carolyn responded in the tradition of throwing the disappointment and guilt first.

"I know, Mom. It's not like that."

"And he's hurt you before!"

"That was a long time ago," she answered, knowing her mother was right. "It's fine. Nothing has happened. We're just talking."

"I heard he just got divorced. You need to leave there now!"

The fact that her mother knew Jason's marital status that was just over a year old surprised her. Jason's parents were deceased, along with most of the community her parents had when living in Cleveland. The rest were living in diminished capacity at a senior facility in an adjacent community. Maybe Carolyn learned the news from one of Callie's sisters? Maybe one of them was keeping tabs on Jason to ensure he never crossed paths with her again? Social media made that easy to do.

None of those thoughts mattered to Callie. She wanted to return to the present to finish her weekend. She had learned so much about the man she released decades ago who did not come back. It was important to her to finish her time with him at the beach.

"I can't leave," she replied strongly. "You don't understand. Everything's fine. Trust me."

"You've put yourself into a very bad situation," Carolyn warned. "And, what about him? You need to be careful! Don't do anything you'll regret."

The comment was legitimate. But it still angered her to hear it from her mother. Prior to her Saturday arrival, she would have agreed with that statement. But, now that she had spent time with Jason, had some really open discussions with him, and met one of his children, she saw again the man she loved as a young adult in the man that was now a dad in his mid-fifties. Her anger toward him was gone. Life had worked out for both of them.

"You know him. You know his family," Callie replied, trying to place guilt on her mother for thinking the worst of her.

"I know how he treated you long ago. You're doing something that can—"

Callie had heard enough. Carolyn's point had been made and her disappointment with her was clear. But she was at the beach with Jason in a setting that felt safe. It was clear he still had feelings for her; and she likewise for him. Those feelings, however, came with counterweights on both sides that were influencing what could evolve. His were less than hers. But both sets were critical to their lives beyond themselves.

"It's all fine, Mom. I'll be a good girl. I promise," Callie closed in a calm sincerity. "Bye, Mom."

Callie hung up and stared at the water nervously while rerunning the conversation in her head. She felt relief that her trip was no longer secret to her most trusted confidante. Over time, she knew her mother would grow to accept the good that was coming out of this weekend's visit. How much time that would take remained to be seen. As Callie continued to try to link together how Carolyn learned about Jason's divorce, he sat down next to her.

"Maya's gone," he said, with mild disappointment.

Callie stayed silent while still working the links in her head.

"Callie?" Jason asked while extending a bottle of water trying to get her attention.

Callie jerked back from the approaching bottle and into the present. She smiled, a bit embarrassed by her reaction.

"Thanks," she commented, while removing the top for a drink. "Maya get off OK?"

"Yes," he replied, curious about her state of mind. "Is everything OK?"

"I don't know."

A sudden feeling of anxiety kicked Callie to her feet. As she walked toward the water, she turned to Jason with a defeated expression.

"Oh, my mom says hi. She knows I'm with you because I JUST TOLD HER."

Callie was hysterical as she showed Jason her cell phone. She then turned to walk away.

Jason neither moved nor replied as she turned away. He was unsure if she needed to either walk that off herself or if she wanted compassion from him. His immediate urge was to run to her side. But he could see she was dealing with something where he was the agitant. Any effort to either comfort or support could be explosive to her as she worked through what just happened with her mother.

Jason waited a few moments and watched as Callie squatted down in the wash of the surf while breaking into tears. Her back was to him as she held her hands to her face. He was waiting for a moment of calm that would be open for an approach. As she stood to stare out over the water, he decided that was his opportunity to go to her.

"What's going on?" he asked.

Callie turned to him with an unexpected smile on her face. Tear marks streaked both cheeks and her eyes were red from crying. She was shaking as she stood in the wash of the water.

"I just confessed to my mother that I'm here with you," Callie said, calming from the hysteria. "I threw it at her like a little kid proud of being bad. Not just bad, REALLY BAD. Like 'I want to get caught with you' BAD."

The importance of that statement was clear to Jason. Callie's relationship with her mother and father was extremely close. She was also the third of three daughters. And her pureness and innocence on the outside sometimes met with a demonic fire that she would use to push the envelope on their rules to test their patience, particularly with statements meant to incite them. Jason knew her confession was as much for that as it was to release the building pressure within her that she could not confidentially share with anyone else. Not even Sandy.

"What'd she say?"

"To be careful," Callie replied stoically. "Careful! And to leave right away... Not do anything I would 'regret.'"

"Have you?"

"I don't know," she replied, succumbing to tears again. "This has been wonderful, truly wonderful. That should be wrong by itself! You've been so good to me. Maya was so nice to me. I feel so relaxed. Well, not now, of course..."

Callie threw her hands up in frustration. From his experience raising daughters, Jason saw this one action as positive, knowing that the release of the tension was the tipping point to the calm needed to work toward a solution.

"You needed this weekend. It has been good for you," he said calmly. "And it's been good for me too."

His words surprised her. Her first thought was that he was trying to exploit the situation to pull her closer.

"We have families," she replied, exhausting herself of air as if in a last attempt to keep him at bay. "I have a marriage. I have children I would die for, who wouldn't understand any of this. This would crush them. This would mess up their weddings. What am I doing here?"

Jason did not respond to her question. He knew the swirl of conflicting thoughts and emotions that were going through her mind. It was something she had to work through herself to have the confidence to make whatever direction she would choose work for her happiness.

"Do you love me?" she asked him in a quiet tone.

Jason smiled, recalling the first time he saw her.

"I've loved you since the moment we first met," he answered, taking a step closer. "I remember it like it was yesterday, where we were, what was said."

"Are you in love with me?" Callie interrupted.

"I won't answer that right now," he replied, while taking both her hands in his.

"Why not? It's a simple yes/no question. Are you in love with me?"

"I... I adore you," he answered while searching for the words to express the truth without saying it. "You were the only girl I asked to marry me on the pure fact that I couldn't live without you."

Callie smiled as the words tumbled toward her. That thought had never occurred to her until now. Stephanie was pregnant when Jason asked her. That was 'obligation' even if they were 'tracking' that way. Callie's engagement to Jason was based in 'want,' which was refreshing for a moment until she remembered that it did not happen.

"That was a long time ago, and you did!" Callie responded as her tone turned angry. "You ran away and did live without me. You raised a family WITHOUT ME! And that's not what I asked."

"I'm sorry," Jason replied. "It's not that simple."

"Why?"

Jason tightened his grip on her hands to ensure she would stay for the whole explanation. His eyes gravitated from the sand at their feet back to hers.

"Because what if... WHAT IF.... what I say makes you stay here?" he said. "Then, all of a sudden, you decide that you want what you left in Washington... back? That just won't come back together, Callie. You'd have ruined that because of what? Two days? With me? In this fantasy land?"

Callie understood his words, having thought through all the things he was explaining. It irritated her that he thought he could just win her back through a weekend at the beach. Twenty-seven years had passed since they last saw, let alone touched, each other. Families had grown up around both of them during that time. Two days compared to twenty-seven years was not going to make her abandon her current life for him. Still, she wanted to know.

"I just want to know what YOU want," she asked. "Want me to tell you what I feel?"

Jason could feel the conversation heading to a spot that it should not reach at this point in their rediscovery of each other. It was being driven on pure emotion, which was dangerous.

"You know what I want," he replied. "And no. I don't want to know."

"Why? Aren't you happy I'm here?"

"I've dreamt about this."

"Then what's the problem?"

Jason's immediate thought was how to explain his position without sounding like he was preaching a process to her. He felt her eyes on him as he looked off to find inspiration on how to lay out the process that he felt she needed to go through instead of running purely on the emotion of the moment.

"You have a lot to figure out and to do for yourself before there could ever be an 'us'," he answered.

His words reminded him of the 'stage setting' he would do with his daughters, which felt weird.

"What are you talking about?"

Callie was growing impatient with his tactical, almost condescending, response. They turned to walk back to their chairs as Jason prepared his thoughts. Callie's eyes watched him work through the details as she did back when he used to disappear into his own head mid-conversation because something sparked something else that had to be worked out. This time, however, it was not funny. It was important. But she knew it was worth waiting for.

"You have twenty-seven years of life since me to work out," Jason answered, while looking off into the ocean. "That's as much for you, as it is for your family, and frankly, for me."

Jason turned to look at her, finding her eyes focused on each step she took as the waves washed over, then back off, her feet.

"I've done some critical things that you haven't," he continued. "First, I came to realize that trying to make everyone happy at my expense was making everyone miserable."

Jason knew Callie's level of commitment to her family, faith, and word superseded any personal desire to be happy. Her personal integrity was built on that foundation. It was why she tolerated him for so long during their engagement when things started to disintegrate. But she had to know that the ripple effect of unhappiness is strong. It is a contagion that can spread quickly and overwhelm everything. Her mother, her children, and even her husband ultimately wanted her to be happy so that they too could be happy.

"Next," he added. "I got a divorce from my wife for no other reason than the relationship was over."

Jason waited for that to sink in. From what he could tell, his experience was different from hers. His marriage was over before it started and lingered through the four kids out of obligation and a desire for him to be with his girls through their entire childhoods. Although, at times, things looked promising with fun nights and happenings, the bulk of the time was just spent doing what needed to be done to get from one day to the next. From what he could tell from Callie, her life was more fulfilling than his had been without her.

"I then reconciled with my kids, which was hard. But it's OK now."

Jason knew this was the biggest obstacle Callie was facing. If Chase had already left her, then moving on to something new and together would be an easy decision. Her children, however, were another story. The expectation that they have no clue and that they prefer unhappy parents to stay together fighting was wrong. As his kids matured, they saw the nuances they had missed in their younger years. And despite the fact that divorce creates disappointment initially, it does calm over time if the parents put the children's needs ahead of their own.

Jason thought about his oldest daughter Rachel's initial response of 'It's about time' when he and Stephanie shared with the collective group that their divorce was happening. Elise and Faith were tearful at the news and did not address it much during the process. Maya was the most animated, expressing hope that they would decide to work out their differences for the sake of the family. She avoided Jason's outreach for months after he moved out. They rekindled their relationship when he visited her freshman year for a fall football game while down touring cottages to buy at the beach.

Jason watched Callie as she listened to what he was saying. It was unclear if she agreed with him. Her non-response to each point was unusual.

"Anything less than all that happening would make anything that could evolve between you and me a cheap affair," he added. "I won't do that to us, and I certainly would never make that part of your legacy."

Callie finally gave a slight smile in appreciation of his integrity.

"Finally," he finished, as her expression started to fade again. "I moved here to be away from there. And, if I'm laying all my cards on the table, to be close, and accessible to you."

Callie took several moments to rerun his final confession through her head. She had been processing everything 'family' that he was saying to build her own picture of conversations and responses that would happen if she left Chase. *Close and accessible to her* was an unexpected wrench in the machine that shocked her and brought her thoughts to a standstill.

"Close to me?" she asked in complete disbelief. "That's bullshit. There are a lot of beaches closer to DC than this one. You moved to North Carolina to be close to Maya, and likely more for the in-state tuition."

Jason smiled at her reply. It was a confession he did not want to make that just found itself attached to his sermon on his life's transition. But it was now out there. Like Callie's confession to her mother about being with him, there was a relief that came with telling her how he ended up on the Outer Banks rather than on a beach farther south or north.

"That's the public story," he answered. "But I knew... hoped, that my being here would find its way to you, and that it would be an easy add-on to a trip to your mom's IF, and only IF, your life was heading where mine went... I couldn't just reach out for you."

Callie sat down in the beach chair to think about what she had just heard. She knew she just got the answer she had asked for earlier. But the reality of the effort and the expense for him to get there was substantial. He moved his life on the chance that she was miserable and would come find him.

"I didn't know if you'd come," Jason admitted, taking a seat next to her. "What I know of your life didn't give me any hope that you would."

"Appearances can be deceiving," she answered, not even thinking about the words.

"Yes, they can be," he replied. "Tell me, did you ever REALLY think about me until you saw my post? Ever?"

Callie sat quietly as she listened to his question. Her eyes were focused on a distant object crossing the horizon. The enormity of Jason's confession was still overwhelming her. Twenty-seven years of no contact and he moved to the North Carolina coast to be close enough to her mother hoping she would come looking for him.

"That tells me a lot," Jason continued, disappointed in her non-response. "I'm beginning to think my great plan was a stupid one."

"Yes," she answered quietly toward the sea.

"Yes, what?" he replied, still locked on disappointment. "Stupid plan? Of course—"

"YES!" she repeated, turning to him. "I'm kind of ashamed to admit it. But I did... and I do, more often than I want to admit. And I shouldn't have. I'd see your soccer posts on Facebook that you were literally down the street from my neighborhood and would drive by just to see if I could find you to see what you looked like in person. I even parked and 'walked' some of the parks hosting those tournaments, IN THE RAIN, looking for you. How stupid is that?"

Jason took Callie's hand, working to console her guilt while also grateful to hear her confession.

"I wish that would've happened for us," he responded. "Maybe a little divine intervention that it didn't. I knew the same thing and looked for you everywhere we ate and shopped. I couldn't just drive by your house though."

Callie smiled, picturing him cruising by her house with one of his kids. Her house and neighborhood were not what you could say you lived in during your twenties.

"That's funny," she answered. "I just have so much to think about."

Jason released her hand as she was not returning his grip. It was obvious her mind was teetering back and forth from fantasy to reality. But there was a reason that she was there that centered on her happiness with Chase and the life they had together. He wanted to help her work that through.

"I don't know your husband," Jason started, getting a startled look from Callie. "He could be the greatest guy on earth or a complete douchebag. But you're entering the stage in life that Steph and I hit a few years ago. When Maya was heading out, we looked at each other and knew we wanted different things that didn't include each other. It was actually kinda funny... until it wasn't."

Callie's initial response of surprise was followed by silence. Jason was not sure if she was listening. But he had one point to make that was his driving force through his divorce. She needed to hear it in order to set her compass to what was right for her versus what she thought everyone else wanted.

"You only live once," he said quietly to catch her attention. "And you need to work this out for what YOU want... I'll be here. Or at least somewhere you can find me. But YOU HAVE to make decisions about your marriage and family first. We, as in you and me, can't even be a speck of consideration."

Callie was comforted by his words that she would always be able to find him. Her expectation about her life as usual dampened the thrill of his interest in her. She did not want Jason to be alone. In the same light, she also did not want him with anyone else. It was a crippling dilemma. Her immediate response was to just look up and to smile.

Jason knew to talk anymore would work against his effort for Callie to find peace and happiness. He knew, at best, she would stay through noon tomorrow, which gave them precious few hours left to talk and to enjoy each other's company. Callie was still processing everything, which was taking away from their time. He had to get her to shift gears.

"Let's just have fun for the rest of the day and tonight," he said while slapping his hands together to bring her back to the moment. "You can hit the road home tomorrow when you want."

Callie smiled as she began feeling some emerging fun coming. But one detail lingered in her head that she wanted to clarify.

"So, when you said at the gas station when we first saw each other that my being here wasn't a coincidence..." she started.

"I set all of this up hoping you would come find me," he finished. "But the choice had to be yours. I honestly didn't have high hopes it was going to work."

"What was your plan if I didn't show?"

"Well, there are lots of beach moms around..." Jason responded.

Callie forced a smile as she visualized Celeste on Jason's arm at an Aborigine happy hour. The sight made her cringe and jealous. As she tuned back to him, his face flashed to a devious smile that she remembered from long ago and knew that anything that was said with it was bullshit.

"Seriously," she said, seeking some level of honesty.

"I don't know," he replied. "I guess wait until you no longer go to Williamsburg?"

The comfort and pressure created by his statement fought within her. She felt an adoration for the man she had previously loved and hated at the same time. He was sitting inches from her wearing a smug face that she wanted to both smack and to kiss. She often felt guilty creeping on his social media just for a glimpse of him over the years. She then pulled her thoughts back to the present as her internal clock told her that the weekend was going to end.

"Speaking of Williamsburg," she said, "I'll have to leave early to have time tomorrow to see... rather... to face... my mom."

The collapse of Jason's time window to an earlier departure disappointed him. Her reason, however, was necessary as part of her process to return to her home to figure things out.

"That's fine. I'm sure it will be fine," he replied, trying to give hope for the conversation Callie was on a collision course to have with her mother. "Maybe I'll ride up with you and the three of us can do brunch?"

The devious little girl in Callie appreciated Jason's comment as she thought how Carolyn would respond to Jason trying to hug her. Her lips curved to the smile he was seeking. But the practical mom quickly returned as she came to grips with the fact that Jason being anywhere near any of her family would be explosive.

"It probably would've been better if at the gas station we both looked at each other and said 'eh'," Callie stated.

"That never crossed my mind."

## 19

The group of Abbies gathered on the beach was smaller than the night before. Despite Monday being a holiday, some had returned home for either work or school obligations that disregarded the man and events that led up to the discovery of the 'new world' that hosted their little strand of paradise. The sun was already sitting behind the homes, casting growing shadows onto the dune and shoreline. The music playing was classic 1970s Jimmy Buffet. Zoe and Molly had already raced off to run with the other dogs and kids near the waterline as Jason and Callie arrived with their cooler of refreshment.

Rebecca looked up and smiled to see the arriving couple. Although still concerned about the wake to be left behind Callie when she finally left, she was happy to see her with Jason, who seemed happier than usual as he greeted some of the others on his way in. Jason asked Callie to wait for him as he left to place their cooler with the others in the community pot. A collection of free drinks that was open for everyone and often led to debates about who skimped, and who had the best drinks to target.

As he set his cooler onto the sand, Jason was cornered by the dad of the girl he fished from the surf earlier in the day. Although happy to talk to him, he quickly looked to Callie to ask for a moment with the grateful dad, which she granted with a smile.

Still feeling like an outsider, Callie took the moment to enjoy watching Molly run with Zoe and the other dogs. It was a controlled chaos that worked with few collisions and no growling. She knew Molly would run to the point of complete exhaustion, then collapse for a good night's sleep.

"Heyyyyy," called out through a familiar Southern accent. "I wasn't sure I'd see you tonight."

Callie knew before she turned that the voice was Rebecca's. She took a pull from her cocktail as Rebecca approached, expecting to field some questions, and maybe some warnings.

"That makes two of us," Callie replied while feeling a sweet twinge of booze fall through her body. "Nobody's home at my house. So, I might as well enjoy one more night of this."

"I'm glad you're here," Rebecca answered while reducing her voice to a sarcastic whisper. "The conversation's kind of stale with the small numbers."

Rebecca smiled after her comment, then lit up again. Callie felt an ease build within her that seemed to only come to her when acquaintances transitioned to friends. Friends you feel you can trust as things unfold around you in life.

"I don't know if I'll be much fun," Callie said softly.

"Just be yourself," Rebecca replied. "We're all friends."

Rebecca's words reminded Callie of her comment to Jason about not being there to make new friends. It was true at the time. But she appreciated the fact that her attitude did not determine the success of becoming friends with Rebecca.

"So, how's the weekend been for you two?" Rebecca asked cautiously, and deliberately, through her cup as she took a sip of drink.

Callie watched Rebecca's eyes not lose contact with hers. Rebecca's interest was more than just casual conversation. It was positioning to see how things were evolving so that she could be where she needed to be as the final acts unfolded through tomorrow.

"If I'm being honest," Callie answered. "It's been really stressful... but also truly wonderful."

Rebecca listened and shook her head in agreement as she pondered Callie's comment.

"I can't imagine what you're going through," she commented.

"I don't even know why I'm here. Being lonely and unhappy but having a family is one thing. Being completely selfish and taking a huge risk to spend innocent time like this with a love that failed long ago is just stupid," Callie confessed.

"Curiosity is a really powerful force," Rebecca replied, then paused to think. "You know, I really like you."

Callie was thankful to hear Rebecca's confession. Her concern for Jason was real and obvious. There was no reason for her to feel anything but concern about Callie being there.

"That's nice of you to say," Callie responded cautiously. "I like you too. I also feel a BIG 'BUT' coming."

Rebecca found the *big but* comment funny as she put together what she wanted to say to her new friend. Over the twenty-four hours since first meeting Callie, she was growing conflicted as her concern grew from one friend to two.

"Yes," Rebecca answered, changing to a slow, serious tone. "All I ask is that you don't give him false hope. He's obviously really into you. Likely set this all up to get you here. But that happy success is also very sad for him in its own way."

Rebecca regarded Callie and Jason as a passing romantic rekindle that was going to burn fast and hot, then burn out. She also saw it burning one of them badly, if not both of them, in the process.

"He has had no interest in any of the single woman here who are quality and really like him," Rebecca added. "Really fine women. And some not-so-single ones too. Those are better left alone."

Rebecca rolled her eyes, adding to her sarcasm. Many homeowners had commuting husbands who would arrive late week and leave on Sunday. Some of their wives did not like being left alone, which Callie related to immediately. Rebecca finished her thoughts with a seriousness Callie had not seen from her before.

"BUT," she said, with emphasis, followed by a smile to deliver her promised words. "What I can read about him is that he wants the long term with the person he calls 'his one.' He thinks we all have one. And I think his is YOU."

Callie blushed at Rebecca's observation. Its warm wash through her face was something that she had not felt in decades. The last time she remembered feeling it was when Chase expressed more than dating interest in her, which reaffirmed her personal confidence that she could love deeply again. Callie was embarrassed by the obvious color she was showing, which confirmed Rebecca's belief that their weekend likely was not going to end well.

"I want that too," Callie confirmed. "I'm just not sure who that is for me."

Rebecca did not respond, knowing Callie was not looking for suggestions. Callie was also at a loss for words that she found particularly frustrating. Both started to look for an exit when Rebecca's face lit with an observation.

"Well, my new friend," she smiled. "I have good news. And that good news is that you don't have to decide anything today, or tomorrow, for that matter... AND we have alcohol."

Callie smiled as Rebecca lifted her glass to release both the conversation and the tension that was all around them. Together, they turned from the water's edge to return to the group. As Callie scoured the party for Jason, she found him standing alone between them and the group watching them they walked toward him. When she got close, she nestled next to him, grabbing his hip from behind as he wrapped his free arm behind her shoulders.

The doctor mindset in Rebecca was in full motion to know all sides of the situation. She knew she was far from done with her survey as she watched Jason and Callie work their way back through the group. Most of their conversations started with a pat on the shoulder for Jason in honor of his heroics earlier in the day. Rebecca was amused watching Callie's response that started with pride for her man then quickly transition to eye-rolls as the topic kept repeating from conversation to conversation. As Jason could only be Jason, he listened politely through each person's recount then tried to change subject. Rebecca's moment to get him to herself happened when he separated from Callie to refill their drinks.

"How's it going?" she asked as she presented her glass for a refill.

Jason's timing to refill their drinks required Rebecca to chug the last half of her drink to set up their coincidental meeting at the coolers.

"Fine?" he answered cautiously.

He was suspicious of Rebecca's question. History had shown her questions tended to dive deep before any awareness happened.

"Are you OK?"

"Of course I am," he replied. "Why do you ask?"

Rebecca looked to see if Callie was occupied. She was not surprised to find her looking at them while involved in a conversation with one of the other Abbie moms. Rebecca knew her time was short. So, she cut to the chase.

"Look, Jason," she said as he turned toward her. "We've only known each other for a few months. But it's not hard to see that something far more than just a friendly catchup weekend is happening here."

"And you... disapprove?" he sniped back quietly.

"That's not my place," she answered. "But Callie's married, which is so dangerous in so many ways. I just don't want to see anyone hurt here, especially you. This may have started innocently. But we both know it's not going to end without pain. I just don't want you, my very special friend, to hold on for something that may never happen."

Jason raised his eyebrows to confirm receipt of Rebecca's concern. He then smiled and patted her on the shoulder as he walked away without saying a word.

Later, as the party dispersed, Callie hugged Rebecca and thanked her again for being so friendly to her and such a good friend to Jason. Both had tears in their eyes, realizing that their conversation was likely going to be their last. Rebecca hugged Jason a little longer to support her good friend as he set off with his 'one' for their final hours together. She waited to watch them ascend the stairs and disappear out of sight over the dune.

#

The thud of their noses hitting the glass could be heard at the bench area as Jason and Callie returned to the cottage. Callie reacted with a motherly concern while Jason laughed at the two bewildered dogs as they turned to look back for their owners.

It was well past Zoe's dinner time and all the exercise from happy hour had increased her hunger. Likewise, Molly added her own smear to the glass as she waited in anticipation of her overdue dinner. As all four entered through the sliding door together, the dogs scampered to their bowls to be disappointed that food was not waiting.

Callie put her glass on the counter as she sat down on a chair to relax. Jason worked through his normal routine of dumping out the cooler on the deck and returning all the bottles and cans to their rightful place to be ready for the next go-round. He then turned to feed the dogs.

"That was so fun and so easy," Callie declared, while looking up to the ceiling fan for air flow. "I can't remember the last time I went to a party that wasn't either political or full of condescending people trying to one-up each other."

Jason smiled and looked over at her as she spoke, appreciating her not only for her presence but also for the life he had with his friends there.

"That's just human nature, honey," he remarked before stopping abruptly. "I'm sorry. That just came out."

Jason immediately went to her as she began to tear up. The comment was so natural, yet so wrong. It had blown over her unnoticed until he pulled it back with his apology.

"I can't believe this is going to end," she cried softly, using a napkin to wipe her cheeks.

Jason reached for her hand to comfort her and was rejected when she put her hands up.

"What?" he asked, confused by the action.

"I've hugged you, kissed you, have had urges to make love to you," Callie whimpered. "That's insane. We've been apart twenty-seven years! Why all of this now?"

Jason was stuck for an answer that would make any sense.

"Life changes?" he remarked, embarrassed by the clinical thinking. "I don't know. I think it's natural to have those urges, especially when you're hurt and mad. But we didn't do anything."

The qualifier, he hoped would give her solace, did not work. Her internal conflicts were coming to a head as time was ticking down and decisions, she felt, had to be made. To carry on a parallel relationship with him was unacceptable to her and to each of the men who loved her. The pressure inside her was building.

"I slept with you."

"We slept in the same bed."

"God, I want this," she said, looking around the quaint little cottage decorated with a heavy male influence.

"You can't decide that now."

"Why are you pushing me away when you can have me?" she asked. "Are you self-destructing again?!"

Jason smiled at the well-intentioned jab. He knew it was rooted in a history of pain giving her a legitimate reason to ask. Was the weekend playing out to their past? Did Jason build something, succeed, and now be working to end it?

"No," he answered, taking her hands in the two of his. "I want you to stay, but for forever. I can't take the short term on this. And it is nice to know you don't hate me anymore."

Callie showed relief at his answer. There was a truth in it that made her believe he was sincere. She began to laugh as she realized the meaning of his last comment.

"I never hated you," she said. "Well, not for any real length of time."

Their confessions were disrupted as the dogs clamored to be let out. Jason opened the sliding door, allowing the two to run to do their business in the sand. Zoe had a spot that Jason knew and could find to dispose of anything left at sunrise. He hoped that Molly's pattern of doing everything Zoe did would make the search-and-disposal effort in the morning easier.

"Look at those two," Callie remarked, watching them through the glass door as they disappeared down the beach stairs. "Molly's never been this crazy and happy. And I never would've let her out to just run... in the dark... at the beach."

"Well, I'm sure Nantucket has its rules on that," Jason answered sarcastically before thinking.

"You had to spoil it. Didn't you?"

## 20

The box that held the remains of the pizza they ordered sat on the deck next to the bench. A bottle of cabernet sat next to it with its cork pulled. The night was again perfect with warmer than usual temperatures and the onshore breeze that kept the bugs away. The blanket they shared covered their shoulders as each stared off thinking through their own thoughts on what is, was, and could be.

"Penny for your thoughts," Jason asked Callie, as she remained still beside him.

"I'm just thinking through the shit-storm I'll face when I see my mother, and then when I get home," she answered as she reached for her wine.

"That's what you want to think about now?"

"I can't help it," she replied.

"Do you really think they know?"

"I don't know. My mother certainly does. I made sure of that!"

Callie took a large pull of wine from her glass as Jason situated to comfort her.

"Your mother won't betray you."

"No, but she'll certainly let me know that she doesn't approve," she replied. "And she'll do it for a very long time, like she did when I told her you and I were having sex while dating."

"Oh my God," Jason replied, stumbling through an unexpected laugh. "Wh-why would you share that?"

Callie backed away from him, shuffling both arms and legs in a confused effort to move.

"I don't know. I was mad, hurt," she answered. "Does it matter?"

"Yes... well, no," Jason replied as he thought it through. "I guess it makes me wonder what she thinks of me."

Callie looked at Jason with a complete look of disbelief. He had not seen Carolyn in twenty-seven years. He was now fifty-five years old with a family of his own. She was not even sure her mother would recognize the current, salt-n-pepper person he was today.

"She'll want me to stay with Chase because I married Chase, have been married to him for twenty-five years, and have three children with him."

Callie rattled the line items off like a church liturgy embedded over years of repetition.

"What about love?" Jason asked, looking for a ray of sunshine.

"I do love him," she answered with a brutal honesty that hurt. "How can I not? I married him and had children with him. They're my family. Jesus! You're NOT helping me!"

Jason took her hand again.

"I'm sorry, Cal. I can't."

"It's not fair, you know!"

As Callie cried out, she tossed his hand aside to stand to face the rail and water.

"It's not fair that you're here, available, and so perfect for what I need now," she continued.

Jason saw an opportunity to pull Callie back toward him but decided that her emotional state would likely lead to decisions that could be harmful to them later. *Long term. Think long term*, he kept telling himself through the moment.

"But how about tomorrow? Next month? Next year? This is just a start that gives you something to think about. I'm not going anywhere," he answered instead.

Callie turned to him and smiled. There was no pressure from him on her. She was there of her own free will. She knew he would let her leave if, and/or when, she ever chose. She returned to her seat on the bench next to him.

"You have to figure everything out for you," he said calmly. "Your kids will still love you no matter what."

"What if I decide to stay with him?"

"Then you'll be happy," he answered.

Jason held a smile through the pain of the statement as he reached to move a small strand of hair off her brow.

"I promise."

The silence of the night was filled only by the sounds of the recurring waves washing against the shoreline. Jason woke to Zoe's moan as she shifted position next to Molly who was nearest the bench. Callie was asleep, nestled comfortably into his chest and shoulder. She had always been a sound and peaceful sleeper. Beautiful in her innocence and vulnerability.

As Jason moved slowly to lift her without waking her to carry her back to the house, both dogs stirred to attention. In a single move perfected when putting his infant girls to bed, he elevated Callie in his arms as he further nested her into his chest. She made a cute, slight murmur as they moved as one to stand. The next hurdle he saw was the sliding door, which he had little confidence he could get through cleanly.

The door proved to be less of an obstacle than he expected. He opened it slightly to allow the dogs in, then finished with his foot, back and butt to make enough room for him to get through with Callie. Although he remembered Callie as a sound sleeper, his thoughts were that the wine was helping to keep her asleep as he slowly progressed down the hallway and into the guest bedroom.

As Jason laid Callie down onto the bed, she readjusted into a fetal position to face toward him. He then placed a light cotton blanket over her.

Jason took a moment to watch her sleep. He then pinched another small strand of hair that was resting on her cheek and set it behind her ear. He knew he could watch her all night. The moment was too perfect to leave.

"I fell in love with you the first time I saw you," he said softly as she slept in front of him. "And I'm more in love with you right now than ever before. I'm so, so sorry."

Jason waited a few moments to watch her before leaving as quietly as they came in. He closed the door halfway to give Molly in and out access. When the light from the hallway dimmed, Callie opened her tear-filled eyes, knowing she had heard the words she asked for.

The expectation that he would sleep was ridiculous, and he knew it. Anytime Jason had anything of either opportunity or worry, the last thing he could do was sleep. Zoe was settled into her usual spot at the foot of his bed. Molly was nowhere to be seen and thought to be in Callie's room. Jason could see the gap he left in the guest room door was still there. He expected that Callie was still sound asleep because of the exhaustion of the day, the emotions, and the wine. He felt happy for her to find the rest she needed before heading back to DC.

As he watched the fan spin above him, his door wisped open as Callie walked in again, wrapped in the blanket from her bed. Without saying anything, Callie laid facing him with her eyes wide open, darting around his face. As her eyes settled, she smiled before lightly touching his temple. A light kiss on the mouth followed before she pulled back to study his face again.

The kisses that followed were more passionate and grew heavier with each ensuing touch. The coolness of her mouth heated as the pressure of each connection increased. Her hands washed down from his face to his chest that inflated to her touch. Neither of them was thinking as they moved to touch limb to limb, and torso to torso.

Callie pushed Jason onto his back and rolled up on top of him. Her mouth rarely left his as they both stretched to maintain contact with the other. As her hands cupped his shoulders, she sat up pulling him along with her. Sitting on his lap with her legs next to his, she removed his shirt to rub her hands on the chest she had been wanting since seeing him at the gas station. She leaned into him to push him back to the bed as she stayed upright. After a brief pause, she removed her shirt, exposing the chest he remembered first seeing in her parent's house after a day of swimming. Her body was as beautiful now as it was then as she pressed her flesh against his. He could feel her heart pounding and as it synchronized with his.

The pleasure was intense. More intense than any moment he had experienced since her. The drive to keep going was undeniable. They were both in the same moment, feeling the same connection. To complete the most intimate connection was driving both of them. What was going to happen was unquestioned until Jason stopped them.

"As much as I want this. As much as I've dreamt about this. I can't let you do this," he said, working to catch his breath through each word. "You'll regret it. And you'll hate me for it."

"Shhhhh," Callie answered, putting her right index finger gently over his lips.

Jason relaxed as Callie relaxed softly on top of him while gently rubbing his chest. Her skin next to his skin was what he remembered. The warmth of her body, her chest, and her breath. It was the perfection he remembered and ached for when their hearts and passions would reach rhythm before and during lovemaking. Stopping did not shortchange the experience for either of them.

"I just want to feel your skin on mine," she said in agreement with his thoughts. "I want to feel your heart beat again with mine. The way it used to."

Jason pulled her closer as she calmed to a still. Callie was relaxed, fully aware, and content that she was in this position with him. He kissed her forehead to fill the moment and held her until she was asleep in his arms.

## 21

Chase listened to the mowers completing their work on the course as he sat on the villa's terrace. It was just after sunrise. The rest of the house was still sleeping off the previous night's debauchery. The final tee-time of the weekend set for 10 a.m. That would put him on the road by 3:30 after lunch and prizes. He would be home no later than seven.

Callie had been an early riser since she and Chase met. It became more embedded after having children, having to move them out to school during the school year then off to camps in the summer. Callie never slept in unless sick, which was rare. Chase took a chance that she would be awake and called her. When his call rolled to her voicemail, he grew concerned that he was still on her shit list and felt he needed to do something notable before heading home.

Chase took a moment to consider his options. Callie was less than two-and-a-half hours from him at the beach. But that was off in the wrong direction. To show up at her friend's house uninvited and unexpected would be fatal for him because of the embarrassment Callie would feel and the distrust he would be showing. He decided instead to call Carolyn. Williamsburg was halfway between Richmond and the beach. If it worked with his golf time, he could drive to there to surprise Callie on her drive home.

"Hello?"

"Hi, Carolyn. It's Chase."

"Hi, Chase. You're up early," she stated, suspicious of the call so early in the morning.

"I know, I knew you'd be up," he apologized. "Is this too early?"

"No, I'm just reading the paper," she answered honestly, having Sunday's *Washington Post* spread out across her granite countertop.

"Has Callie returned from Stephanie's?"

Chase felt embarrassed to ask, disclosing that his wife was keeping him in the dark about her location and timetable.

"Stephanie's?" Carolyn answered. "No, I expect to see her on her way through later today."

Chase hesitated to follow up with the question that had been nagging him all morning. His searches on social media had not given him any insight into who Stephanie was. After her divorce finalized, Jason's Stephanie changed back to her maiden name on everything to include her social media. Her online connection to Jason was only reflected in the court records: one of marriage and later, another one of divorce. Chase could not hold back his curiosity.

"Is Stephanie related to Jason Cartwright? They have the same last name."

"That's a name I haven't heard in a while, Chase," Carolyn lied, while pushing down all surprise in her voice. "Stephanie Cartwright? Maybe. I'm not sure. Why do you ask that?"

"Because they have the same last name?" he answered while growing anxious. "Is that coincidence? His sister?"

Carolyn nervously moved the *Post* around her countertop while constructing an answer that would be truthful without selling out her daughter.

"I don't think they're related, Chase," she said, knowing their divorce was final. "You two can talk when you get home. I know she's driving back today."

Chase got no satisfaction from Carolyn's answer. Callie's relationship with her mother was unbreakable. Her mother had an uncanny instinct about her that could sense problems, then go into hyper-protective mode to make sure the impacts of those problems were minimized. Callie had a propensity to generate more problems than her sisters, which made her relationship with her mother particularly close. Chase was reluctant to just sit and wait when so many things looked and felt out of place.

"I suppose you're right. Thank you," Chase said to close the call. "Enjoy your paper."

Carolyn shuffled through the sections of paper on the counter as she hung up the phone. Next to the editorial page was a file full of photographs she had pulled from the family albums but kept as a history for her girls to go through when the time was right for them. On top of the stack of photos was a casual picture of a younger Callie and Jason together, enjoying a laugh at a Labor Day dinner on the golf club's terrace in Cleveland. It was Carolyn's favorite picture of the two.

Next to the picture was the thank-you note Jason had written to Carolyn and Callie's dad when they crossed paths not long after the engagement broke. The message was short and affectionate. It took considerable time after their split for Carolyn to look at that picture with any level of warmth and affection. But that feeling did eventually return for her. She hoped it would someday return for Callie, too.

As Carolyn continued to wonder through all that was happening, she returned the photo and note to the file. She then returned the file to its spot in her desk in the kitchen.

# # #

Chase remained unsettled after his conversation with Carolyn. She seemed apprehensive and slow to answer his questions. The coincidence that Stephanie and Callie's first fiancé would share last names was the most nagging. Cartwright was not an uncommon name. But it also was not as common as Smith. With the house still quiet, Chase reopened his *Find My Phone* app to get Callie's exact location at the beach.

It only took a few moments for the map to home in on Jason's block to put a blue dot on top of his beachfront lot. With the street name written next to the dot on the map, Chase then googled real estate transactions for owner names on the street, hoping to learn more about whose cottage Callie was visiting.

As a list of options slowly loaded on his phone, he bypassed the advertisements and clicked on the first link to the Dare County real estate tax office. He entered the street name that ran the coast of the county resulting in a list of owners equally long. As Chase scrolled down a Google map of the community, he found a pier Callie's location. He clicked on the pier to get its street number. With that number, the list of over a thousand names just shortened to about one hundred. The real count depended upon if the house numbers went up or down heading north from the pier.

Chase returned to the real estate records window he had set aside and began to scroll the owners within reasonable distance of the pier's street number. It was only moments before he found that Jason Cartwright was listed as an owner of a cottage about where Callie was staying.

Infuriated, Chase googled *Jason Cartwright Cleveland*. As the results loaded, he noticed a *Cleveland Business Times* article appear with the caption *Kiva Global buys Backlit Marketing for $50 million*. Under the caption was written *Founder Jason Cartwright to remain as a consultant*. Chase stared at the caption with the realization that Callie was either with Jason or with him and his wife Stephanie.

The next Google listing was presented in straight type. It was the published legal divorce notice in the *Cleveland Post-Gazette* of Jason Cartwright from Stephanie Cartwright last year.

"Fuck," Chase whispered to himself.

He immediately stood to go pack. As he quickly piled his clothes into his bag, his roommate, Sabby, woke from the noise. Sabby fell out of bed to quickly dress to a level of decency needed to go after his friend. He had been wary of Chase since Saturday's call with Callie and knew that something was imploding on him. He knew he needed to calm his good friend back down.

As Sabby ran out onto the front walk of the villa, he discovered he was too late. Chase had already grabbed his clubs and ripped out of the driveway. The lead they had going into the final day of their golf weekend had just been flushed down the toilet. Sabby decided that it would be best to wait until later in the week to call his best friend to find out why he left so abruptly. He then went back to bed.

## 22

The leaking sunlight repeated its daily ritual of working its way across the room when Callie woke topless to confirm the night she remembered in Jason's bed. As she tried to jostle free from the blanket, the familiar weight behind her was again pinning down her release and again refusing to move. And like the day before, her bladder woke with her and was now screaming.

Callie had little patience for the dog that was impeding her trip to the bathroom and took a blind swing of her arm to move her off the blanket. As she felt the impact of her strike against the dead weight behind her, Jason jumped and fell out of bed with a thud.

"I thought you were the dog," Callie laughed, while still tangled in the blanket.

"Usually is," he answered, while climbing to his knees to lean against the bed. "I wasn't in the mood for a swim this morning. I didn't sleep well last night."

"What'd you do?"

"I watched you," he answered softly with a warm smile. "You're so peaceful and pretty when you sleep."

Callie smiled to the comment as she sat up in bed. The blanket fell from her shoulder to expose her chest. Undaunted, she stretched, reaching her hands high and pushing out her breasts. She finished her stretch by running her fingers through her hair. She did not pull back to hide her exposure and did not return the blanket for coverage.

"How'd I get back into the blanket?" she asked, rolling toward him.

"You were shivering," he answered. "I put it back on you to get warm."

Callie gave a soft smile for his thoughtfulness.

"I have had two really good nights of sleep here,"

She rolled closer to give him a kiss. The touch of her lips sparked competing feelings of delight and pain because of not knowing if this was the last day of their journey together. Her mood showed potential for more.

"That's a bonus," Jason observed, trying to be cavalier. "You'll go home well rested."

The words were out and recognized before he could stop. Callie's expression dropped all its happiness as the reality of the dream coming to an end was just given its final timeline.

"I'm sorry, that just came out," Jason moaned, trying to reclaim the lost happiness.

Callie stood, remembering she had to pee. With no attempt to cover herself, she walked out of the room, half naked, to find the bathroom.

"It is the reality of today, isn't it?" she answered.

Jason slumped onto the bed, angry with himself that he had killed his final minutes with her the same careless way he killed his opportunity for a life with her. When he heard the shower start, he knew their affectionate time was over. He stood to get dressed and to start breakfast.

## 23

Jason worked quickly to pull together a complete breakfast with a nicely set table before Callie was finished dressing. It was likely the last meal he would share with her. He wanted a final opportunity to share life visions with her to see if there was potential that she would ever find her way back to him again. All that was fair for him to expect now was her possible interest and hope. She had a lot to consider. Her personality and history made betting against the two ever sharing time together again an almost certain win.

Callie appeared in the living room rolling her packed bag and dressed to go. Jason was surprised given the time it would take to get to Williamsburg and back to DC. Even with holiday traffic, leaving the beaches, along with the drive back up I-95 to Great Falls, Callie had time to spend with him before heading home.

"I didn't expect you'd be rolling right away," he said, still preparing breakfast to guilt her to stay.

"It's a long drive," she answered. "I have to stop to see my mom."

Callie's tone showed that her visit with her mother was going to be painful. She regretted sharing her secret with her the same way she regretted using her house as a pitstop on her way to the beach. In hindsight, it would have been better to stay in Great Falls over the weekend with Netflix and Molly. But, when she looked at Jason, dressed in shorts and a t-shirt along with bedhead pushed down by water he must have pulled from the kitchen sink, her regret turned to gratitude. She was thankful she had taken the time to rekindle their friendship and to re-establish a love that had gone dormant but was never truly lost to either time or mistakes. She wanted to hug him and to stay. But she knew it was time to go.

"I'm about to make breakfast," Jason declared, desperate for anything to keep her there. "We still have some doughnuts."

Callie's eyes moved to the table where Maya's box of pastries sat. She could see Maya's first expression when they first met and her scorn and disapproval as she discovered who Callie was. It seemed unnatural that she and Maya should have connected so easily after their first encounter. That gave her hope that no matter what happened between her and Chase, that Lizzie and her brothers could come around to not only accept a decision to end her current marriage, but to accept a new person as her mate.

"Maya," Callie smiled, still holding the mental picture of her. "She's great."

Jason felt a twinge of hope with Callie's recollection. He watched her take a doughnut out of the box as he delivered two mugs of coffee to the table.

"I'm sure I'd say the same thing after meeting your kids."

"I don't know," Callie replied. "Maya has a maturity and confidence my daughter doesn't have... that I don't have."

"Maya's been challenged with a lot of things kids her age shouldn't see. I know you have incredible strength. I've seen it. Your kids likely do too."

Callie forced a smile of agreement to the statement. Her confidence was low, given all the circumstances in motion. Even if no one was aware of where she had been that weekend, she had a lot to think through. If anything leaked to anyone or was uncovered, a wildfire would erupt in her life that would be devastating.

"I suppose you're right," she replied.

"I know."

Jason words ended with a smile as he held up his doughnut as a toast. Callie laughed at the absurdity as she raised her doughnut to his.

"We would have had beautiful children," she said, as she touched her doughnut to his.

"We have beautiful children," he answered, extending his doughnut to her mouth.

Callie responded with the same instinct to feed him as if the doughnut was wedding cake. They both missed the other's mouth leaving doughnut residue on their faces. First, they both laughed at the sight of the other then dropped to blank expressions at the realization that their wedding never happened, and their weekend together was now over.

"One last look at the ocean?" Jason asked, as he wiped Callie's mouth with a napkin.

"Sure."

#

The GPS read that Chase was under ten miles from his destination as he crossed the final bridge onto the island. He changed apps to check her phone's position. It still had her at the house owned by Jason Cartwright. He then scrolled back to the GPS screen for final directions.

#

As they arrived at the bench that hosted most of their time together, Jason took Callie's hand as they looked out over the water. Families with small children were walking the beach, likely for their final time until next year. Zoe nosed open the gate to give Molly one final run on the sand.

"This is heaven," Callie stated into the breeze as she watched the family with small children hunting for shells. In her mind, she replaced the adults with a younger Callie and Jason.

"I don't know about that," Jason replied. "Salt... sand... sun."

His smile grew through the alliteration of the words. Callie's expression, that was sad as she turned, erupted into a teary smile showing that her sadness to be leaving had left, if only for a second.

"I have to go back to my real life."

"I know."

"If it were just me..."

"I get it," he said to stop her. "Really, I do."

"Promise me you won't stay alone waiting for me to come back," she said, her voice cracking with emotion.

Jason smiled in response and called the dogs to return. Together, the four walked back to the cottage.

## 24

Jason carried Callie's suitcase down the stairs, recalling two nights earlier when she stormed out and dropped it to bounce down into the sand. As he looked around, the two cars he saw under his cottage represented two diametrically opposed lifestyles. One that he left. And one that fit him better. The Range Rover's tailgate opened as if sensing their arrival with luggage to load. Jason pushed the button and watched as the tailgate closed on his dream weekend with his 'one'.

Callie stood still silently as she waited for Jason to finish. As they walked together to the driver's door, he reached into his pocket. Callie opened the door, then turned to say goodbye.

"For whatever you need, if ever, whenever, you need it," he said, while handing her a card with all of his contact information.

Callie studied the card for a moment, then looked to him.

"Thanks for our weekend, for being so understanding, and..." she paused to hold her emotions. "For being a gentleman."

Jason smiled in appreciation for her words, taking a deep breath to stop from crying in front of her.

"You're welcome, and... it wasn't easy."

He surrendered to holding back his tears as he hugged her tightly. She returned his affection with the hug he remembered that pulled on and hurt his neck. It was a pain never forgotten and forever to be cherished. As they separated, Jason finished his thought.

"Thank you for coming, for making my weekend and my summer."

"It's fall," Callie corrected, bringing laughter to the moment.

"My year," he added, not happy that the length of time was big enough to express his appreciation.

They both then fell silent to search for more words to say.

"I really appreciate you stopping things last night," Callie said to break the silence. "I guess I'm turning self-destructive too."

Jason studied her face as he contemplated his response.

"That's not self-destructive," he replied. "You're just trying to figure things out. We knew how we fit when we split. It was killing me to know who you became."

"And?"

"You're everything I..."

The pain of watching him stumble through the emotions of her leaving completed Callie's renewal of her love for him. A love that was set aside, ignored, and even, at times, forgotten for decades as she found someone new and created a family with him. The tough, stoic, young man she knew had finally exposed his softer side to her. A perspective that may have been hidden when she loved him decades ago. Or a trait that grew in him through his marriage, family life, and four daughters. Regardless of how and when, she saw it in him now, at a time when she needed someone who wanted her.

"Will I see you again?" she asked, gently pulling his hand from her face.

"I really hope so," he answered.

Callie took one last look around the parking area and sand leading to the dune. The cottage was the perfect romantic getaway for empty nesters. But she knew that the beach, even with all its appeal, would lose its luster over time, making the action of a big city like Washington attractive again. She wondered about Jason's plans to stay, not just for the coming winter, but the longer term.

"Will you stay here?" she asked. "Or is this project over?"

Jason understood the reason for the question. Despite never having been a big fan of the sun, the sand, and the salt, the community became his own and The Abbies became his friends. He did not know if he would try a winter on the North Carolina coast. But, to him, it did not matter.

"I'll be where you can find me," he answered, as he kissed her forehead.

Callie shuffled her feet as simply something to do. Her eyes darted from his to around the parking lot and out onto the street that would take her from him.

"I don't want to go," she said, reaching out for a final hug.

"Thanks for coming and for trusting me," he replied as he pulled her to him.

Callie hugged him tightly again, then released her hold. Jason held on a little bit longer. She then climbed into the driver seat, started the engine, and closed her door as her window rolled down.

"Stay in touch?" she asked.

Jason's response was just a smile as he backed away from her car. Callie's look of sadness was completed by the tears on her face. As she started to back out, Zoe and Molly appeared as if to not be forgotten.

"Oh my God," Callie laughed, while still in tears. "I almost forgot Molly."

Jason opened the door behind her to load Molly. He grabbed Zoe's collar to keep her from joining her new friend for the ride back to Washington. As Molly settled into her usual spot on the front passenger seat, Jason closed the door.

"Zoe's going to miss her friend,"

"Isn't it funny how they got along so well," Callie replied, to delay her departure just a little bit longer.

Jason smiled at her comment while visualizing a table full of their kids sharing a meal.

"I wonder," he replied, "if our kids would do as well?"

Callie smiled as she visualized the expected craziness in her head. She threw her hands up in an imagine-the-thought gesture. She then put her hand out of her window, beckoning him to come closer to share one last soft kiss. Jason pulled back first from their final touch with a smile as Callie shifted into reverse and started to back out. Both gave halfhearted goodbye waves.

## 25

The sound of tires grinding sand disrupted their peaceful goodbye. Callie stood on her brakes, stopping the Range Rover inches away from Chase's Maserati as it slid to a stop behind her. The shock and surprise of the event pulled Jason's immediate concern to Callie to ensure she was okay.

As Callie settled from the surprise and jolt of the panic stop, Jason turned to investigate what made a car skid onto his driveway at a high rate of speed. As he turned, a blur came at him making any defense purely instinctive. He released Zoe from his grasp as he started falling with what just struck him.

"Shit! CHASE!" Callie screamed, as she watched him jump Jason beside her door.

Callie's scream gave Jason immediate perspective on who just attacked him as they both fell off the concrete parking surface into the sand. The force of the tumble separated their bodies, enabling them both to stand. Jason positioned himself for another run from Chase as he reoriented.

"Calm down," was all Jason could say as he held his hands up defensively.

"Calm down!?" Chase answered, while regaining his balance and collecting his breath. "You spend the weekend fucking my wife and I'm supposed to calm down!?"

Callie jumped out of her Range Rover and grabbed Zoe, who continued to bark. Callie's 120 pounds struggled to keep Zoe's seventy-five pounds from shredding Chase's leg. Molly joined Zoe, barking through the driver's window that was still open.

"Chase! Stop!" Callie yelled, as he attempted a wild swing at Jason to stumble to his knees on the soft sand.

Jason grabbed the back of Chase's shirt and pushed him face down into the sand, pressing down on his shoulders to keep him from moving.

"Stop it," Callie demanded. "It's not his fault."

Jason gave Callie a puzzled look while he continued to press her husband's face into the sand.

"You're talking to him. Right?"

"Yes! Chase!" she said, trying to calm down from the excitement. "It's not Jason's fault."

Chase stopped fighting Jason's hold and held his hands up in surrender. Uncertain of his intent, Jason released his hold to let Chase stand, fully expecting him to come at him again. As Chase stood and began shaking sand off, his eyes never looked up. As expected, Chase started toward Jason, again ready to fight.

"Stop!" Jason shouted, with his left palm out and his right fist cocked. "Or I'll drop you."

Chase stopped his approach, seeing what was about to come his way. Out of breath and bent over, he turned to Callie, knowing his ability to hurt Jason Cartwright was over.

"What the fuck, Callie?" he pushed out, while gasping for air. "What are you doing here?"

Callie looked at her sand-covered husband in his bright golf attire, white footie socks, and loafers struggling to breathe. She was caught red-handed at the scene of her crime. Her only defense was the truth. She knew it would hurt him.

"Originally?" she answered, in an angry tone. "To do exactly what you think I was doing... with someone who wanted to be with me... even if just for a weekend."

Jason evaporated from her consciousness as she focused on Chase. Chase was hurt and humiliated in his failed attempt to defend his rights and honor as Callie's husband. It was a pathetic look that Callie had never seen in her normally confident and strong DC political strongman.

"Did he invite you here?" Chase asked, looking for reasons beyond him for her actions. "Can't keep your own wife, or find a beach wife, so you take mine?"

Chase looked again for opportunity to start towards Jason. Jason's left-hand palm went up slightly, along with his right fist that was again cocked and ready to fight. Callie grabbed Chase's shirt to stop what she knew would happen if her soft-in-the-middle campaigner took on the swimmer.

"No," she confessed, feeling no guilt or shame. "I found him, on Sandy's Facebook. I had no idea he would be here, be alone, or even see me... or be nice enough to let me stay."

Chase secured his footing within striking distance of Jason as he listened to his wife's explanation. He then wiped his face with the sleeve of his shirt. He was thinking he could take him. But Callie was his main concern.

"Of course, he'd let you stay," Chase responded. "Free ass for the weekend."

"Watch it," Jason demanded, in a tone that clearly communicated that Chase's insulting comments had to stop.

Jason tried to remain quiet through the skirmish to not incite things further. He knew any assault on Chase would trigger a protective instinct in Callie against him. His only win was to defend himself from Chase's attacks without hurting Chase in the process. But Chase's digs on his own wife, on Jason's *ONE*, were pushing his limits of resistance to beat the shit out of him.

Both men stared at each other as Callie's eyes darted back and forth between them. Both were thinking through actions that Callie knew she had to stop.

"I also had no idea that he'd tell me to go back home," she interjected, breaking Chase's focus on Jason.

"What?" Chase asked, as if he did not hear what she said.

"Nothing happened here," Callie responded. "I just visited an old friend."

Chase's face changed from confusion to disbelief as he shifted his attention from his wife back to her suspected new lover.

"An old friend? Yeah, right. AN OLD LOVER's more like it," he snapped, then couldn't resist adding "Your FIRST lover. So, that's NOT what this looks like!"

Callie took the assault in stride. She deserved it and knew the statement to be true. The weekend did look and smell like an affair. And it could have been had Jason not stopped the events of the night before. But, going into her visit, the two of them getting to that level was not part of her plan. She had no plan. Her reason to visit was a calling that just happened.

"Well," Callie answered, looking for the right words to put Chase at ease. "You'll just have to get over that. And you're such an asshole for even saying it!"

As Callie thought through her response, her husband had attacked her personally as if her life before him was improper.

Jason was the man she had planned to marry and would have married. That would have eliminated Chase from her life had it not been for Jason's meltdown just before the wedding. She was neither ashamed nor proud of their sexual exploits prior to the wedding. But she was furious that her husband would use it so hurtfully.

"I can't believe you're here. I really can't," Chase said, running his hand through his tussled hair. "You lied to me, to your mom, to Lizzie! for God's sake! Is this what you want? THIS!? Look at this place. You think this is better than what I give you?"

Callie was embarrassed and angered by Chase's arrogant assault on Jason's home. He had no right to demean Jason's life when he was told the choice to be there was hers, and that the weekend was clean of impropriety.

"It's not about the things!" Callie pushed back.

"Yeah, say that when your things aren't there, when your precious Range Rover is replaced by that piece of shit."

Chase threw his arm to point at the Wrangler as he looked back and forth between them. He was calming down, which cleared his thinking to make better arguments under the cottage.

"You son of a bitch. That Range Rover was your idea. You insisted I have it. I was happy with the Suburban."

It became clear to Chase that his angry assault on Callie was not working. The rage that was within him was subsiding to anger he could manage. Her words were eroding his confidence that he was completely right, and that she was completely wrong.

"You're scaring me," he mumbled, trying to find some daylight.

"You should be scared," Callie replied, glancing over at Jason for support. "Nothing happened. How'd you even find me?"

"Your phone. I tracked your phone."

The invasion and distrust reignited Callie's anger again.

"You tracked my phone!?" she shouted. "You untrusting son of a bitch. If anything, I should be tracking yours!"

Chase laughed nervously at the insinuation.

"Perfect thing to say when you're caught with your ex-lover at the beach."

Callie stood shaking in anger as Jason stepped closer to the feuding couple. Chase's look showed that another assault on Jason was likely imminent.

"Stop!" he said calmly, seeing no end to their sparring. "You two do need to talk. But not here with everyone watching and listening."

He then pointed up and out from under his cottage to the decks of homes filled with spectators watching the fight unfold. It was time to put the attacks to bed, to be thought through, calmed down, and discussed rationally another time. It was the same process that enabled him and Stephanie to resolve their differences, separate their things, and move on with their lives.

Callie and Chase looked around at the faces staring back at them. The story had the potential to become headline news and even community lore as the Maserati husband attacked the Beater Jeep Beach Dad to protect his claim on his Range Rover Wife. It was time to end the show.

"Why do you fucking care?" Chase demanded, as he turned his attention back to Jason. "You got what you wanted."

"This is where I live," he responded. "Most of these people are my friends. And, dude, you have no idea what I want."

"It's pretty obvious to me finding you two here," Chase challenged.

"You're wrong," Callie reiterated. "I found him."

"Right," Chase replied, looking directly at her. "And I'm supposed to believe the person who lied to me, her mother, and her daughter all weekend."

"I'm your wife!"

"Are you?" Chase said, looking away then back at her. "This certainly screams otherwise."

"You bastard," she answered, clenching her fist, ready to attack.

"What's your fucking angle?" Chase asked Jason. "You have my wife all weekend and now you're encouraging us to talk? What happened? Not what you expected? Throwing her back again? That's rich."

Chase expected that his reference back to their broken engagement would enrage Callie against Jason again. It was a question to Jason meant to hurt her.

Jason exhaled heavily before answering. Chase was digging himself deeper into a hole.

"You just assume we picked up where we left off?" Jason replied, to expose his naivete to the situation. "If you think this is because of either me or her, you'll never get what happened here. And you will likely lose her because of it. That's what's *RICH*."

Callie immediately looked to the ground away from both Jason and Chase as Jason's declaration sank in. The weekend's revelations were eye opening, not just to the person Jason had become, but also to who she was. Maturing through life and family had refined them both to better people. She wondered if she was too close to Chase to see the changes in him—good and bad.

Jason made no attempt to deny Chase's suspicions that his intentions were to win Callie back. As a master manipulator himself, Chase continued to think through how his wife of twenty-five years ended up there with her former lover. Their last argument about his work travel and choice of his boys' weekend over being with her did not cross his mind. The fault laid with Jason first and then with Callie. Jason had to have coerced his wife to visit. She, otherwise, never would have looked for him.

"You're so fucking arrogant," Chase declared, as he stared at Jason who was within arms' reach of his wife. "I should kick your fucking ass right now."

Jason struggled to hold back his amusement. But the man was pushing the limits of his patience.

"I'm standing right here." he said, to invite another go without moving into any defensive position.

"STOP IT CHASE! Just, stop it," Callie yelled as she turned to Jason. "You too! You just have to take our word that nothing happened."

Chase stood down, then shook his head in disbelief.

"Your word?" he mumbled. "Why should I believe anything either of you say?"

"Do you think I've never thought the same about your 'business' trips with your female staff?"

Callie felt an eerie relief to have verbalized her worst fear for the first time.

"Well, I have. I just never said it."

Chase looked off in disbelief at the accusation as Callie glared, waiting for his denial.

"You also never caught me with anyone..."

Callie's chest deflated with his nondenial.

"Yes, Chase," she answered. "Caught. How would I catch—"

"Stop," Jason interjected.

The debate was not going to end. But the show for his neighbors and the bleeding from their marriage had to. Jason stepped in dangerously close, within sucker-punch distance of Chase, to keep them from further annihilating each other.

"I can't believe I'm fucking refereeing this," he mumbled. "You two need to stop and breathe. Use the windshield time alone driving back to DC to really think about what you want to say to each other. Callie was about to leave anyway."

Neither Callie nor Chase responded to Jason's declaration. Both knew it was time to stop. The question that remained was where to go from there. They both needed to cool down.

"Look, I'm going to walk away so you two can get on your way," Jason continued. "But I'm first going to hug your wife, as friends do, to say goodbye... Don't jump me."

Jason's farewell hug to Callie was to be a sign to Chase that there was nothing between them. A hug that she likely gave to all of Chase's friends, and that Chase gave to all of his friends' wives. Innocent. Appreciative. Healthy.

Chase was hesitant to let Jason anywhere near his wife, let alone touch her. But he knew to object would infuriate her more. He reluctantly granted permission with a hand wave. As Chase watched Jason take hold of Callie, Jason hedged his bets with a comment to his best friend.

"Zoe, watch him."

Jason did not take his eyes off Chase while he hugged Callie one last time. Callie smiled as he let her go and was teary with the realization that this was their last contact.

"I'm glad we had this time together," Jason whispered, which released a wash of tears from her.

"Me too," she answered, barely audible. "I hope you find your 'one.'"

"I have," he smiled, as he wiped her tears with his thumb. "Goodbye, young Callie."

Callie hugged him one last time. She then walked back to her car as Chase kept his eyes on Jason. As she settled into the driver's seat of her Range Rover, she waved one last time to her first love.

"I know who you are, what you have, and what you think you can take," Chase said to Jason in a low cadence as Callie watched from her car.

Jason began to feel sympathy for the man who stood defeated in front of him while trying to hold on to the wife he should lose. He had met Chase's type before, many times. Narcissism about themselves, their jobs, and their possessions made them who they thought they were. He knew that person because, to a degree, he was that person in his earlier life. But he had grown out of that mold long ago, realizing that there was more to living than acquiring and dominating.

"Callie doesn't know anything beyond what she sees here," he replied, to reassure Chase that he was not going to compete.

"Just stay the hell away from my wife."

Jason smiled at the declaration for he knew he could win her given their weekend and what he had just witnessed. But Callie was not his to take. She had a lot to unravel and to calm. And that would take time. He knew any effort to force it would fail. Nature had to run its course.

"I'm not going to take your wife," he reassured Chase. "But, if she leaves you, she knows how to find me. And I WILL NOT repeat the mistake that GAVE you your life with her. It's your call."

Jason's delivery was firm and believable. His observation of Chase's temper led him to add one final point before ending their talk forever.

"Oh," he said, pulling Chase's attention back to him. "If you hurt her in ANY way, I'll fucking shred you."

Chase did not respond to Jason's threat. He knew that Jason would live up to protecting Callie with whatever he had. Chase returned to his Maserati without a look to Callie, knowing she and Jason were sharing their final moment through her windshield.

Chase started his car to its usual high revving punch. He pulled out onto the street as Callie backed out to start her journey home. Jason waved one last time to his 'one' before turning to walk back to the cottage stairs. He watched Zoe make the climb before he touched the first step. He stopped to think as he looked at the sand mark where Callie's bag had landed two nights earlier.

"Wait!"

A warmth flowed through him as he turned to catch her in his arms. Chase stopped and stepped out from his car to watch his wife run to Jason. Helpless, he watched, from a distance, as she jumped into the arms of another man. As she surrendered her hold, she stretched up to kiss him lightly on the lips before letting go.

Jason did not move as he watched the Range Rover disappear out of sight. The weekend was over. He looked for Zoe who was waiting at the top of the stairs ready to move on with her day. He took one last look around him. The decks that had been full of spectators had emptied to a few as a police car drove by. Jason waved his appreciation for their attention, then started up the steps.

The emotion of the moment overwhelmed him as he walked toward the water to touch the bench where he and Callie spent most of their time together. As he looked out over the view they both enjoyed, he found Rebecca on the sand looking back at him. She gave a shoulder-raising, palms-up shrug to ask for the outcome. Jason halfheartedly returned the gesture with a pained smile. Rebecca's response was immediate disappointment for him by mouthing "I'm sorry" followed by a look of sincere disappointment. Jason waved his appreciation to her as he sat down on the bench and buried his face into his hands.

The weeks following Callie's visit became less active and emptier as visitors to the beach tailed off dramatically in late October and through November. As Jason expected, he did not receive anything from Callie despite the many private ways she could get a message to him if she wanted to.

Fortunately, for him, the silence that he and Zoe had grown used to changed when his four daughters all came, as promised, to visit their dad at his little beach cottage for Thanksgiving. Their presence and laughter rejuvenated the life and familial chaos that he loved as the mouthwatering smells of their holiday dinner of thanks made everyone hungry. This meal was Jason's first attempt at managing the complete effort, which he was excited to tackle, albeit with a bit of fear he would undercook something.

As each daughter held to their conflicting positions on how to prepare different parts of the meal and who was to sit where, Jason took a moment to watch and be thankful for the children he had, despite its cost. As he enjoyed their continued chatter, he reached to touch the framed picture mailed to him by Rebecca that he placed on the kitchen countertop. It was the perfect capture of him in the soft October afternoon light during the best weekend of the year.

All four of Jason's daughters noticed the new, prominently placed photo on his counter. As the three older daughters unsuccessfully pressed him for details on who was cuddled and smiling next to him, Maya played along to keep his secret. And beyond enjoying the gamesmanship of keeping Callie's identity a mystery, Jason was happy to see their interest and excitement about his progress to find someone new. As their questions intensified, Jason's phone chimed to save him from their inquisition as well as to say something was ready. When he checked, he found a text from Callie: *Please wait for me.*

MILO HAYS NOVELS

TWO ONCE THERE

Continue Jason and Callie's story with *Two Once There*

Two Once There is the sequel to *Two Once Removed* where Callie Larson and Jason Cartwright come together again as life continues to move forward and unravel at the same time. Through their journey, more truths uncover as their extended families make their realities more painfully clear.

In the months that follow their impromptu weekend of rediscovery and Callie's cryptic Thanksgiving Day text saying to "wait for her", Jason invests in a mountain retreat after staying there over Christmas and New Years. The purchase is kept secret as he suspiciously travels back and forth to Asheville, North Carolina near where the retreat is located.

With her kids on vacation in Nantucket with her soon-to-be ex-husband, Callie makes her return to the beach searching for Jason. Her trip is intended to be a surprise after holding her promise of complete silence while she focused on resolving her marriage issues to a final decree. When she arrives at the beach, Callie only finds his daughters who immediately recognize her as the mystery woman in the photograph on Jason's kitchen counter.

The events that follow draw in family and friends to both combine and collide into a new reality for both Callie and Jason. Their agreed absolute silence, followed by missteps, misunderstandings and a single family tragedy, challenge their destiny to be together to not be as absolute as first thought.

Two Once There is an intense, emotional story about taking the step from mid-life, loveless marriage fantasy to reality. Parents, children, friends and geography add to the blend as both Jason and Callie learn more about what a life together would be and how it would affect them and their lives with their families.

THE GLIMMER IN THE LEAVES

The Glimmer in the Leaves another emotion filled journey of relatable midlife challenges that is a fast-paced, fun, romance story that blends country-club and country at a troubled faux winery with a colorful clientele out in the sticks.

When fifty-year-old Rowan Delaney decided to take a day drive out into the country, his goal was to decompress. The pressures of his high-pressure corporate banking job, his sheltered country club life, and the anxiety of his looming divorce with kids in college were pushing him to the edge. And when his GPS delivered him to a country winery and bar out in the middle of nowhere for a much needed *pit stop* before heading back home, his immediate apprehension turned to intrigue as he was lured past the pick-ups and ATVs in the parking lot by an infectious buzz that permeated out from the building where, inside, sat an alluring new world, a number of memorable characters, and a beautiful, mid-forties bartender, who immediately zeroed in on him with an overly sarcastic welcome.

The Glimmer in the Leaves is a fast moving, page-turning, emotional love story between two struggling mid-life, sort-of singles who find their perfect, and unexpected, opportunity for love in the strangest of places. Trying emotional moments, fun happenings, and uncomfortable run-ins fill the life paths for these two as their two, vastly different worlds find hope out in the countryside, somewhere in the leaves

BRIDGES AND BLIND CORNERS

Bridges and Blind Corners is another captivating story that assimilates the dreams, anguishes, and challenges facing the story's three characters with its setting through the beautiful, rugged, and dangerous coastal terrain of Oregon and California, where *wonder* bridges are needed to span over seemingly insurmountable obstacles, and blind curves bring surprises where deciding what to do happens after passing their points of no return.

Fifty-year-old Jamie Stewart flew to Eugene, Oregon excited to purchase a classic convertible he had coveted since his teenage years. To make it better, he was looking forward to driving it home on a fun, mind-clearing, four day trip, alone, down the California coast to San Diego. But when the seventy-seven-year-old seller asked to join him on his trip, the one she always wanted to take, with her now deceased husband, in the car she just sold him, he does not have the heart to say '*no*' to either her, or to his twenty-five-year-old daughter who joins them in San Francisco when her problems groundswell beyond her control. Three generations. Two very different backgrounds. One incredible journey.

ABOUT THE AUTHOR

Milo Hays' career has been spent telling stories to move emotions. As a fundraising consultant, he worked with wonderful non-profits to verbalize their amazing stories and visions to motive extraordinary levels of giving. As a business entrepreneur, he used storytelling to sell visions for investment as well as to market products and services. One key overlap of both is drilling into the emotional elements of a cause to verbalize it in a manner that touches people and motivates them to give generously, invest, and/or buy. Milo Hays stories are built to exude that same touch where the reader becomes emotionally involved to love, hate, cheer on, and/or cast aside key characters in the stories being told.

"To me, there's nothing better than understanding motives and backstories that drive actions. When I craft characters within a story, their histories have to be rich, their emotions have to raw, and their struggles have to be real. I love it when readers ask for more to a story you think you've wrapped up. That is what makes writing enjoyable for me."

"Thanks for reading my stories. Please visit my website at www.milohays.com if you have any comments or want to look for other stories to read."

Cheers!

MH

Made in United States
North Haven, CT
10 October 2022

25237755R00136